THE
EXPENSE OF
A VIEW

11/10/16

I'm leaving this
as a thank you.
I'll order another
for myself.
The first couple
stories are great.
Thanks for
having me,

Susan

Friendships last longer than presidencies.

Previous Winners of the Katherine Anne Porter Prize
in Short Fiction
Laura Kopchick, series editor
Barbara Rodman, founding editor

The Stuntman's Daughter by Alice Blanchard
Rick DeMarinis, Judge

Here Comes the Roar by Dave Shaw
Marly Swick, Judge

Let's Do by Rebecca Meacham
Jonis Agee, Judge

What Are You Afraid Of? by Michael Hyde
Sharon Oard Warner, Judge

Body Language by Kelly Magee
Dan Chaon, Judge

Wonderful Girl by Aimee La Brie
Bill Roorbach, Judge

Last Known Position by James Mathews
Tom Franklin, Judge

Irish Girl by Tim Johnston
Janet Peery, Judge

A Bright Soothing Noise by Peter Brown
Josip Novakovich, Judge

Out of Time by Geoff Schmidt
Ben Marcus, Judge

Venus in the Afternoon by Tehila Lieberman
Miroslav Penkov, Judge

In These Times the Home Is a Tired Place by Jessica Hollander
Katherine Dunn, Judge

The Year of Perfect Happiness by Becky Adnot-Haynes
Matt Bell, Judge

Last Words of the Holy Ghost by Matt Cashion
Lee K. Abbott, Judge

THE
EXPENSE OF
A VIEW

By Polly Buckingham

2016 WINNER, KATHERINE ANNE PORTER PRIZE IN SHORT FICTION

University of North Texas Press
Denton, Texas

Permissions:
University of North Texas Press
1155 Union Circle #311336
Denton, Texas 76203-5017

∞The paper used in this book meets the minimum requirements of the American National Standard for Permanence of Paper for Printed Library Materials, z39.48.1984. Binding materials have been chosen for durability.

Library of Congress Cataloging-in-Publication Data

Names: Buckingham, Polly, author.
Title: The expense of a view / by Polly Buckingham.
Other titles: Katherine Anne Porter Prize in Short Fiction series ; no. 15.
Description: Denton, Texas : University of North Texas Press, [2016] |
  Series: Number 15 in the Katherine Anne Porter Prize in Short Fiction
  series | Winner, Katherine Anne Porter Prize in Short Fiction, 2016.
Identifiers: LCCN 2016030103| ISBN 9781574416473 (pbk. : alk. paper) | ISBN
  9781574416572 (ebook)
Subjects: LCSH: Short stories, American. | LCGFT: Short stories.
Classification: LCC PS3602.U2624 A6 2016 | DDC 813/.6—dc23
LC record available at https://lccn.loc.gov/2016030103

The artwork used on the cover, *Silver Water*, is by Carol Aust and is used by permission. Cover and text design by Rose Design

The Expense of a View is Number 15 in the Katherine Anne Porter Prize in Short Fiction Series.

This is a work of fiction. Any resemblance to actual events or establishments or to persons living or dead is unintentional.

The electronic edition of this book was made possible by the support of the Vick Family Foundation.

To my family

Contents

Acknowledgments

"Festival" *Witness*

"Three of Swords" *Pembroke Review*

"Honey" commissioned for Facere Jewelry Art Gallery's *Signs of Life*

"Void of Course" *Zone Three*

"My Old Man" *Potomac Review*

"Compliance" *New Orleans Review*

"My Doppelganger's Arms" *North American Review*

"How to Make an Island" *Heliotrope* (Editors' Choice Award)

"Night Train" *Tampa Review* (Pushcart Nomination)

Thank you to everyone who offered feedback on these stories, in particular, Heath Herrick, Steve Cleveland, Barbara Hansel, John Keeble, Gregory Spatz, Rebecca Brown, Carole Glickfeld, Stefani Farris, Nils Coleman, Caroline Allen, Jenny Heard and Rhoda Rice.

Honey

The neighbor is in jail. The words *snitch*, *rat*, and *dead man* and two frowny faces are spray-painted the color of charcoal across his trailer. What idiot thinks a frowny face is threatening? Her laughter, edgily uncontrollable, feels inappropriate. Beside the trailer is a half dismembered motor- cycle chained to cinderblocks, and below it, a large oil stain. Everything has the appearance of having been disrupted and abandoned without warning.

It's April, and the branches of the Siberian elm are lined with golden buds, each a tiny replica of the sun, and the sun is finally warm enough to warm her face. Everything is in transition—the meth head is gone, new neighbors moved into the house behind the trailer, and she herself is a transplant with a new job and no new friends. It hurts to swallow, as if glass is stuck in her throat. It's no surprise she would be getting sick, a danger at the core of any great transit. Last night's bottle of wine hasn't helped. But at least the sun warms even her hands and hair. She's picked up the wayward garbage blown in from other people's yards and col- lected branches and sticks. After a few more slugs of coffee, she'll head to the woodshed for the ax, hoping the exertion of chopping might push away the hangover and illness.

It takes two visits to the woodshed before she sees the dog. She knows it's dead immediately, though there's no bad smell. It looks like it's sleeping—an old Labrador, rust-colored and sweet. Are those shadows on its face or pockmarks where the cheek has been eaten away? Sunlight presses against her back, but the dog is in a darkness and coolness that betrays the day, and the shadows feel tricky and deceiving. She backs up, in case she's wrong, in case it is alive, in case it rises snarling. The dog is like the wasps' nests that line the angles of the ceiling—they shouldn't be active yet, but you can't help but worry. You can never underestimate an injured animal. She closes the door, squints into the bright sun. All the branches seem to wag. A new afternoon wind spins in her ears.

She's pretty sure she saw this dog last week, poised in the empty field between the new neighbor's house and hers, gazing in her direction. She'd worried about her old cat, but then she noticed its paunchy face, the white around its muzzle, its long stare, and the way it stood like old dogs stand, as if it were work. Inside the chill dark house, assaulted by the smell of dirty dishes and cat pee, she searches through small collections of papers for the landlord's card, frustrated by her mess and her inability to locate anything with any shred of efficiency. The landlord, taciturn, says, "Don't have his number." But then, minutes later, the new neighbor calls. He'll be at work until nine. He'll send his son to pick up the dog. He's sorry, he says. The dog's been missing a week. "I thought my ex-wife took her. She hasn't been answering our calls." She does not want to think about ex-wives or the fact that the dog may have been in her shed as long as a week, having crawled in through an old animal door.

She's sitting on the porch step, hopeful she can simply point to the shed, and the son will collect the dog. But the son seems too young to drive, let alone drive a pickup that size. He doesn't know what to say when she rises to greet him. She realizes, looking at his thin face on the verge of adulthood, that this is his first death. It is not her first death. Death is the one thing in which she is most well-versed.

"She's been around most of my life." He pauses as if it hurts. "She's a good dog."

"How old is she?"

"Thirteen," he says. "She's my sister's dog really," as if this will remove him from his grief.

They peer into the darkness of the shed. "What's her name?"

"Honey," he says, "for her color."

She is not honey-colored. Perhaps copper or rust-colored, but not honey.

"I have some tarps I was going to take to the dump," she says.

They fold the tarps into a makeshift gurney. She crouches beside the dog's head, scared of what she might find underneath, maggots, mice? But she cannot ask this boy to lift the head. Honey has not been dead long, which feels like a miracle; there are no maggots, no pockmarks, nothing eaten away, only a small pool of blood where the dog's nose rests. She remembers the fist-sized blood stain that must have marked the moment of her first dog's death, how the next dog licked the stain away. When she lifts Honey's head, she reaffirms the dog's loveliness. She gives her shoulder three pats. Dust rises into the light that now streams through the cracks in the shed and turns Honey's fur her name-sake color. Even the sap beaded around the rings of the stacked wood glows a deep amber color in the fugitive light.

That night she sits on the porch step with a quart jar of honey produced by a nearby beekeeper. She eats spoonful after spoonful, though the sugar will feed the sore throat. She thinks of the man she loved before she moved here, though they never spoke of it. For three years, he inhabited her dreams. They were so connected in these dreams that the waking world, where their union was impossible, felt secondary. "Honey," he said, the night she rested her cheek against his chest, that last night, and did not move away. And then they fell back into their shared silence. A boy on a black motorcycle with a black Mohawk on his helmet whizzes by then disappears into the twilight. Something is coming, but she does not know what.

Night Train

From his upstairs glassed-in porch, Will has an osprey's view of the water surrounding his dock, now lit by an underwater light. He is watching for snook. Some night soon, he is certain, there will be a net filled with a curving silver fish, and until then he can spend his time waiting. Lord knows there's enough time. He fills his wine glass and examines the cut panels of the Waterford alive with tiny street lights. It's hard not to break the goddamn windows most nights, no, all nights. It's hard. You must fill time. Which is why he installed the underwater light last Saturday, a day's project and an evening considering whether it was done right.

Coquina Bay is a dark plate surrounded by a sickle-shaped seawall. In the distance is the loom of downtown St. Petersburg. But here, the lights of houses across the bay are as infrequent as stars. He's been sitting in the window every night for the past three weeks watching for snook. For three weeks he has not even attempted sleep, though mornings he finds himself waking angry in his chair from dreams he can't remember. Mornings white sunlight crashes into his half-opened eyes, and mornings, he kicks the wall, or the other chair, or the narrow, wrought iron coffee table.

The first night after his son's death, he threw a rock at a street-light. One rock. It clunked against the glass and fell to the ground; no glass broke. But now the light flickers occasionally like it's trying to burn out, and he's proud. His office is dark except for sudden flickers of light shining into the porch and casting momentary shadows across the orderly desk, the bookshelves, and the file cabinets. The lyrics to "Hard Times" rattle around in his head. He can't keep these things from moving through his brain: the sound of his dead son's fingers on strings, his cracking adolescent voice, and the lyrics to old folk songs. "What's so hard?" Will used to say. "You've got a great life." Will's father played "Hard Times" too. The seawall and dock are about ten yards from Will's house across a narrow dirt road which dead ends after one more house hidden behind palmetto bushes and fruit trees. Visibility from this height, especially with the new light, is exceptional. Will takes a long drink of wine and watches the wavering green water.

—ɯɯ—

"Willy," his father said. "Don't be scared. It's all light in there, see?"

The cold water from the center of the spring curled around the warm water and wiped against Willy's legs. "It's cold," he said. The warm water was brown, but the spring was green like a swimming pool. Other people stood knee deep in the muddy water. A woman splashed water on her shoulders and arms. Willy and his father were closer to the spring than anyone.

"It's mineral water from a subterranean spring," his father said. "See what a pretty color it is?"

It was a pretty color—bright green, unlike the brown river roped off by red buoys and crossed with the reflections of cypress knees. His father called the knees gnomes, but Willy could never quite see the pointed hats and crooked smiles his father saw.

"What's at the bottom?" Willy asked, looking into the green circle.

"There is no bottom. It's like an underwater cave. Magic down there. A whole 'nother time and place. You could just disappear."

"Uh uh," Willy said, holding his father's hand a little tighter.

"An explorer named Ponce De Leon searched for a spring called the Fountain of Youth because one sip made you young." Old ladies in bathing suits with skirts waded through the murky water.

"That's impossible," Willy said.

"Ponce De Leon believed it."

"Are there fish down there?"

"What do you think?"

"Are there sharks?"

"There are Ichituckni Spring Fish."

"Do they have teeth?"

"Not big ones. But if you take an Ichituckni Spring Fish out of the spring, colors would float up into the air, colors thick as paint, colors so bright they might even stain your arms or your face."

His father touched Willy's nose. "Like this," he said.

Willy looked at his father's finger, but there was nothing on it.

"I don't see anything."

"No?"

Night after night Will watches for the snook. Tonight's no different. The first night he had one glass of wine, the second two, and so on. The red numbers of a digital clock on his desk read 3:03. Three. Three weeks exactly from the day of his son's death. The father son and the holy ghost. BIN 333, was that the number? Anyway, that bottle was at least a week ago. An Australian wine. A night to forget. He made the stupid mistake of going into Jimmy's room. Not tonight though. Nope. Never again. Not going to leave this window spot. Uh uh. The snook will come.

A fucking falling streetlamp. Who does that happen to? Who? Goddamn Jimmy's creativity. Goddamn all his paintings and his musings and his dreams. Goddamn his creepy songs, and goddamn all the music. Goddamn all the music.

—⁓—

The finger picking hadn't stopped. Hours Will had listened to his son playing the same lick over and over. He'd play the lick, stop, play a tape, then play the lick again. From what Will could hear, the tape was some Florida bluegrass guy picking a tune then telling a story. Likely it was someone Will had met as a child, some alcoholic musician who'd drifted into his father's kitchen and drifted out again, some no-name fuck-up who'd left his wife and kid for a night, or a week, or a month to hit the road. Be free. These guys—there was always some other woman, or many of them. There was always a sidekick who'd wave a bottle or a handful of pills and off they'd go.

Jimmy moved on from picking to storytelling. Will heard his muffled voice striking close as it could to that slow Florida mumble. Did he have any idea what he was imitating? If this was any indication of how the first summer after college was to proceed, Will intended on putting a stop to it. College life hadn't made Jimmy more responsible, more capable of waking up each morning prepared for each day, or more presentable; instead, dorm life had made him even sloppier, and indignant—"It's my choice how I want to live," Jimmy would say, leaving a beer without a coaster on a wood coffee table. At least he'd been polite not long ago, inept sometimes, but polite.

Will put his drink down on the coffee table and put *Invention and Technology* face down on the chair. He'd been reading the same paragraph of the same article—about the engineering strategy behind the new Sunshine Skyway Bridge—for over half an hour. He'd grown accustomed to the quiet house of the past year, and if it hadn't been the beginning of the summer, if he hadn't felt, on principle, a need to put an end to this early, if Carol hadn't been napping in the bedroom down the hall from Jimmy's room (though admittedly, Carol praised Jimmy's playing, and she never would have complained—in fact, she'd probably claim the music made her dreams sweeter), and if he hadn't had such an awful, awful headache, perhaps the music wouldn't have gotten to him quite so much. Perhaps he would have done things differently.

He walked briskly up the steps and opened Jimmy's door without knocking, without even thinking to knock. Jimmy, sitting cross-legged on the floor in boxers, the guitar in his arms, looked up, his eyes, squinty and red, his face ashen. He was wasted. In Will's house, with his mother in the next room. With Will downstairs.

"Enough," Will said. "I've had enough of this."

Jimmy stared at him, bewildered, blank. Stoned.

"You do your drugs and play your music somewhere else." It sounded ludicrous the moment it entered the air between them, but too late. He, too, could be indignant.

They stared at each other, and in that stare, Will saw at once his error and his incapacity to admit it. Jimmy was perfectly alert. Emotion moved across his face as it had when he was a child, some dark wave no one could stop, and those tears Will had endured for so long began to flood Jimmy's eyes. Then the bewilderment on his face turned to anger. "Fuck you," he said.

"You keep your voice down. Your mother's sleeping in the next room."

"Get out," Jimmy said. "This is my room. This is my noise."

"Well keep your noise down." Will backed out of the room and shut the door, knowing too well how many lines he'd just crossed.

Downstairs he drank the last half of his drink and poured another, scotch and ice in a tumbler with an anchor on it. He was walking back into the living room when Jimmy came down the steps in a tie dye and ripped jeans. He was carrying his denim laundry bag, his guitar, and a folded page of newspaper. He was barefoot.

"Here," he said shoving the newspaper into his father's surprised hand. Then he left.

The article, from the morning paper Will had left scattered on the kitchen counter, showed a wallet-sized picture of Gamble Rogers, one of Florida's leading folk singers and storytellers, and Jimmy's idol. It was a short article describing his death off the coast of Jackson Beach. He had drowned in an attempt to save a tourist caught in a current.

God, Jimmy had left barefoot.

—ൡ—

Imagine, the last time you see your son and he's barefoot. You don't know it, but he's about to get in a car and drive out onto Interstate 75 and a highway lamp is creaking on its hinges, just as you're saying some biting thing to this kid who you wish didn't scare you so much every time you looked at him, who didn't unnerve the very core of you every time he pulled out the guitar, whose music didn't piss you off and make the deepest part of you regret all you have become. You don't know it, but after you've said this thing you could have said any other day, and after your boy hits the highway barefoot, the light, having already come loose somewhere, like something in you is always in danger of coming loose, this light comes crashing in through your son's windshield. He's going 65, but what does that matter? Except if he'd been going 70, it might have hit someone else's kid.

Pour yourself a glass. Cheers to the window. If he hits hard enough it'll shatter and those pieces of glass will spin through the air like a hundred little streetlights. 3:09. Carol is snoring in the bedroom. She gave up trying to console him two weeks ago. For a few nights she pulled the other chair beside his, in her ever hopeful way, occasionally resting her hand on his hand, on his knee, sometimes touching his neck, rubbing his shoulder or the base of his skull. Her hand felt heavy on his body, and his coldness made her caresses tepid, self conscious, and less and less frequent. Within an hour, he'd forget she was in the room entirely except for the muted gasps of her weeping. He'd stare out the window, alert only to the movement of the green water under the dock. Finally she stopped joining him. Instead, she takes valerian and melatonin and sleeps, a lot.

There are hundreds of versions of Jimmy between Will and the dock, there are moments and there are expressions and there are postures, Jimmy leaning against his VW Bug at a gas station at 3 a.m., his keys locked inside, Jimmy hitting himself in the face, "goddamn I'm lost," walking across the living room, lost, out there, elsewhere, vacant, small Jimmy throwing little, green coconuts off the porch, poking sticks into oranges, standing in the muck beyond the seawall holding seaweed up to his face.

The dark of a palm tree blocks a handful of stars. Jimmy was a weird kid. A real space cadet. You just wanted to shake him sometimes the way he stared. And, god, those dreams. "Daddy, I dreamed I was a fish with a lantern inside me." Will nearly choked when he announced that one lovely morning. All day at work he heard it, "Daddy, I dreamed I was a fish with a lantern inside me," this weird glowing kid, "Daddy," cheers, "I dreamed" where are the snook anyway? "I was a fish" goddamn the laws he'd catch 'em with the lights off "with a lantern" let that quiet the waters "inside me."

———✳———

There were five regulars, the fiddle player, the banjo player who was Uncle Lester, the mandolin player, his father, and another guitarist. Every Sunday all of them would be in the kitchen playing tunes and passing around a bottle of scotch. Willy's sitting on a stool by the screen door, the warm air smelling of jasmine and gardenia and punk trees. They start out slow playing the same thing over and over, but then all the instruments join in and they go faster and faster but you can still hear that same thing underneath. Willy's head feels like a balloon. The music, like a train, makes him empty and anxious, small and alone. His father is speeding away, and he's running after, but the sound of the train is filling his head and his legs can't keep up, and the smoke is obscuring his view and the train is squealing in his ears, and then it's a dot and he's filled with silence. He's staring down at the tracks, wondering at their construction, counting the cross sections.

The fast music stops. The faces of the players are shiny and red. "Damn," Uncle Lester says as he lights a cigarette. The flame silhouettes his mass of wild hair. Smoke rises in the hot kitchen. Willy's sleepy, but he's scared to close his eyes, scared the players might disappear behind the smoke like in a magic trick.

"Hey boy," Uncle Lester says, "ain't you gonna play one of these days?"

"He don't play," his father says. He bends his face to his guitar and picks a short lick.

"Ever tried the banjo?" Lester yells. Willy could have heard him just fine if he didn't yell.

Willy shakes his head. Lester's pale hand is covered with freckles. His face is freckled, and sections of his red, moppy hair stick out while others droop into his eyes. One of his two front teeth is missing, and the lower ones are crooked. He looks like a scary cartoon.

"He don't play, Lester. Pass me that."

Uncle Lester hands Willy's father the scotch. "Huh," Lester examines Willy. "Don't he have your genes, Sam?"

"Guess not," his father says. He tips his head back and swallows. "I'm going out for a smoke."

Some of the other players stand up, stretch. The mandolin player bends down, his face wrinkled in concentration, plays a lick like a jig over and over. Willy hops off the stool, pulls a white mug out of a cupboard, and pours himself some water. He shuffles across the linoleum looking about the kitchen, at the mandolin player still perched on a stool, into the darkened living room where Uncle Lester and the guitar player have turned their backs, and finally through the screen door where he spots his father standing on the porch looking out past the punk trees which separate their yard from the neighbors, and across the low roofs of other small houses. The branches of the live oak rub against the tin of the porch roof. Willy stands under his father's arm which is raised, palm against the house. The other palm is open and filled with colored tablets, red and pale blue and chalky yellow.

"What are those?"

His father turns and looks down. He looks annoyed and surprised. "Oh," he says. "It's you."

The summer night air is hot and balmy and smells sharply of rotting fruit. Across the yard are the dark shapes of collapsed oranges.

"What are those?" Willy repeats, standing on tiptoes so he can see up close.

"What are you drinking?"

"Water. What are those?"

"These?" His father's face is lit by the porch light, his eyes sunken and shadowed. "Magic rocks, from your Uncle Lester," he says finally.

"They are not," Willy says peering closer into his father's big hand.

His father looks him in the eyes, his face slack and frowning. "Why do you always have to be so damn literal?"

Willy steps back against the door frame. Water splashes onto his bare leg. His father puts the pills in his mouth, picks up his beer from the porch step, and swallows. "Magic," he says.

The mandolin player is joined by the second guitar player and then the banjo. His father turns abruptly and walks back into the lighted kitchen. Willy, stunned, watches his hunched back. His father bends to pick up his guitar, sits down on a wooden folding chair, and twists the white knobs that tighten the strings. A bottle comes his way, and with one hand, he takes a long drink, passes it on, then pulls finger picks out of his shirt pocket.

Soon his picking mixes with the others. Willy sits on the floor just inside the kitchen, his back against the doorframe. As the mandolin player's lead fades, his father's guitar picks out a melody Willy knows well and the others follow. *My mother's brother Arthur drove a dovetail Cadillac* . . . His father sings in low tones; the silver picks flick against strings; he counts the strings on the face of his father's guitar. . . . *Then I heard old Arthur yell, if you see me I'm alive, and if you don't you just cain't tell.* His father's face is slack and distant. Willy wraps his arms around his knees and tries to make himself small. Watching his father's bent body makes him ache inside. *Every time I hear the highway call, Lord I feel the years roll away. Turn my future to the wall, Lord and let the tears just fall where they may.* The words roll around in his father's mouth and come out soft and deep. *But a man in love with living don't run easy to the end, the fates may be forgiven once this April's on the wind.* The notes form a body, and the body moves around the kitchen, touches Willy on the shoulder, then floats out into the sweet-smelling night and disappears.

—⁓—

Jimmy ran away once. It started at the breakfast table after a bad dream. Jimmy, his face dark, brooded over his bowl of cereal. Will wondered where a seven-year-old learned such an anguished expression.

Carol rubbed his back. "Jimmy, honey, eat up. You'll never make it through the day without food in you."

Jimmy pushed the corn flakes to the edge of the bowl with the back of his spoon, but they floated back to the middle. He pushed them under the milk and they reemerged. "Why do they keep coming back?"

"Who cares?" Will said. "Eat up."

Jimmy started crying.

Will gave Carol the I didn't do anything what's up with him glance.

"He's had a bad dream," Carol said.

Jimmy got up, picked up his Bugs Bunny backpack, and walked out into the street to meet the school bus. Half an hour later Carol found his school books on his bed. Jimmy didn't come home that afternoon, and when Carol called, she was told Jimmy hadn't been in school all day.

Will drove along the seawall from Coquina Key to downtown St. Pete, the few miles he believed Jimmy could have covered. No Jimmy on the seawall. Downtown, he parked near Straub Park where all the summer concerts were held. It wasn't summer, but Jimmy had weird notions. A homeless man slept on a bench, a dog rooted through a garbage can, but no Jimmy. Will walked the length of the piers downtown. Aisle after aisle of Boston Whalers and Chris-Crafts and sailboats, women in T-shirts and bikinis scrubbing decks, no Jimmy. He couldn't think of any place else, and this is when panic rose from his stomach and into his throat. He stood outside the boat docks looking across the park squinting his eyes, the sun like a needle in the corner of his forehead. His hand over his eyes, he scanned the seawall, the sidewalk, the pier where people were out selling T-shirts and ashtrays and coffee mugs. He scanned the bay itself; no small person with a backpack. Finally, the ache in his head settling into his shoulders, he went back to his car and drove toward Coquina Key.

Where was his son? The brooding, dark face over the cereal bowl, the backpack, Bugs, that's all, folks, got no imagination, work counts for nothing, we're all leaving you. We're all leaving. Jimmy in bed with his thumb in his mouth curled on his side. Jimmy with a mouthful of food giggling at Will's bad jokes. Jimmy holding his hand pointing out boats at the pier. Jimmy on the beach walking face down following the line of the incoming tide.

Will ran a red light. The blood rushing through his body rushed into his head, his head expanding and light like it might disconnect from his body, and the body would run away. Just then, Will drove past Jimmy walking along the edge of the seawall not even a mile from home. He was walking with his head down and his hands in his pockets, Bugs Bunny's face moving up and down with each step.

Will pulled over. The terror that had ebbed into a migraine and a floaty, bereft I can't live another moment feeling turned sharply into anger. The car wheels squealed as he hit the brakes. Cars behind honked and pulled around him. Somebody yelled. He jumped out of the car, slammed the door—Jimmy stopped dead on the seawall—Will took a few steps toward him, grabbed his shoulders tight, as if deciding whether to shake him or hug him. He crouched down to Jimmy's level and held him so he could see him. He looked into Jimmy's oblivious face. "Where have you been?"

"I was in the mangroves—"

It didn't matter where. "Don't you ever—"

"You're hurting me," Jimmy sobbed. "Let go."

———〜〜〜———

Will presses his forehead against the glass of the porch. Sometimes in the evening Jimmy would sit with him by the window, and together they'd point out the Big Dipper or Orion or Venus or the North Star. Jimmy made up the Ear Constellation; Will insisted he wasn't allowed to make up constellations, but

Jimmy'd just giggle. "Too late," he'd said once then kissed his father's cheek and ran off to bed. Song books were scattered all over his floor. There was a painting Jimmy'd done of a train chugging up railroad tracks that ended like a ladder ends in the night sky. These are the things he found in Jimmy's vacant room. When was that? However many nights ago. A train ladder, a track with an end. Little lights in the sky, each drawn as a miniature lantern.

Willy presses his forehead against the kitchen window. He's sitting on the stool he sat on the last night his father and Uncle Lester and all the others played music. The chairs are still in a circle, and the empty scotch bottle is still on the counter.

"He's just in a mood, Willy. Don't worry, he'll be back," his mother says from somewhere behind him. But he doesn't turn around. He just stares out at the dusty driveway and three palm trees poised against the glaring blue sky. It's been a week, it's been two weeks, it's been three. The palm trees are the same. The dust in the road kicks up again and again, but it is never from the wheels of a powder-blue Chevy.

"What is literal?" he thinks, but he never asks. The magic rocks transported his father. Lester took him away. Willy was too literal, so his father left. He'd watched from his bedroom window—his father and Lester arm in arm stumbling across the yard, their shadows crossing the shadows of palm trees. Magic. And now he waits for them to come back.

He and his mother play cards for hours. He watches the circle of his mother's hands dealing: here have luck, have chance, have a diamond, have the King of Hearts himself. He listens to her cry late at night, and late at night he creeps into the kitchen, like some little cat someone forgot to feed, and waits in the window until morning.

There is no moon tonight. There are stars and there are street lights and there are flickers of light on the water. Jimmy's Ear Constellation is out. The wine glass is empty. The bottle is empty. The red clock in the darkened office says 3:21. The green light under the dock is the only bit of color in the night. His net leans in the groove between the pylon and the rail. It's true his father left with Uncle Lester and never came back. It's true he's never been able to remember his dreams. It's true he could never play music, that he was a quiet, skeptical child and that he has grown into a hard-working, angry man with nothing to show for it but an alienated wife, a dead son, and a pretty house. He watches the green spot intently as if it were a cave out of which some answer will swim. The little lights on the water look like stars, and the stars look like little lights.

—·\\\·—

Willy's father sits on the edge of his bed. "Tell me about the night train," Willy says, not for the first time. There is a quarter moon rising above a palm tree outside the window.

"The Celestial Rail ran between the towns of Jupiter, Juno, Venus and Mars," his father says.

"But those towns don't exist anymore."

"That's right. Not Venus and Mars and Jupiter."

"But we've been to Juno. We've been to the beach at Juno."

"Yep, we sure have."

"I like the beach at Juno. Juno has good ice cream. What happened to Venus and Mars?"

—\\\—

"Daddy, tell me about the Star Train," Jimmy says.

"The Celestial Rail ran between the towns of Jupiter, Juno, Venus and Mars," Will begins. A whippoorwill calls in the night.

"It had ghosts in the cars, right?"

"No. But it did take people from the center of the state to the coast to go to the beach."

"But it didn't just go to the beach," Jimmy says. "It's the Celestial Train."

"If you know the story, why don't you tell it?" Will says, and Jimmy smiles then covers his mouth with his hand.

"It was before the time of circles at the end of the line," Will continues, "so the train would go forward one direction and backward the other."

———✲✲✲———

The top of a palm frond cuts through the bottom curve of the quarter moon. "How did it know where it was going when it went backwards?" Willy asks. He thinks about walking backwards and running into things. How can you travel when you can't see where you're going?

"It was a smart train, Willy. A real smart one," his father says, his warm, rumbling voice inviting him on a ride to the stars.

"Did it have two engines?"

"It had a big brain."

"It did not," he says, giggling.

"Sure did," his father says. "It could go anywhere. Thing is, why go anywhere when you're already going to the stars?" A satellite moves slowly across the sky.

"Venus and Mars were towns. They weren't stars."

"You sure 'bout that?"

———✲✲✲———

"Could it fly to the stars?" Jimmy asks.

"Why fly to the stars when it's already going to Venus, Mars, Jupiter and Juno?" Will says.

———✲✲✲———

"Straight one way, and straight backwards the other way," his father says.

—————۱۱۱۱——————

Outside, the light Will hit two weeks ago wavers and blinks. Rock goes up. Rock comes down. Finally, he turns away from the window and looks into the office. It takes a moment for his eyes to adjust to the darkness, but then he begins to recognize himself. There are file cabinets filled with tax returns, paid bills, duplicates of the most important paperwork from the office, clippings on things like the environmental impact of new gas lines on the Gulf Coast and methods of oyster farming in the Panhandle. On his desk are stacks of file folders in one metal basket and invoices in another. There is a cockle shell Carol picked up on the beach with change in it. There is a brass scale.

The blinking light crossing the floor makes his world feel distant as if he were looking at it through water, the gray carpet, the clean, white walls, the charts of Tampa Bay and the Intracoastal Waterway, the old Navy clocks, the structural drawing of the Sunshine Skyway Bridge. 3:33. When he turns back to the window he sees the dark, long shape of a snook cross the green water. Then another. He watches as they gather around the legs of the dock, six or seven in all.

Finally, he walks through the dark room, down the dark hallway, past Jimmy's closed door. He stands in the door of his bedroom for a moment and watches Carol's sleeping body. Her face is turned toward him, and watching her he registers at once familiarity and distance, comfort and disbelief. He walks down the steps, through the living room, and outside. The screen door bangs twice behind him.

The air is damp and warm and smells of star jasmine. A night-blooming cactus flower has opened on a vine looped around the trunk of a palm tree. He crosses the dirt road, under the blinking streetlamp, and steps slowly onto the dock. He picks up his net, lies on his stomach with the net beside him, and peers into the water. The snook have momentarily scattered, but he can see tails and noses around the edges of the light. He waits, and in that waiting feels a new exhaustion. The giddiness of the wine has disappeared; his head feels heavy, and he is dizzy, and there is pressure on his skull. A fish crosses into the light. He watches. Then another fish. Then another. He stares into one silver eye of a fish poised in front of the underwater light. He wants to blink but doesn't. The light makes his eyes burn. He thinks of the way an eye refracts color and light. Does the fish's eye refract color? Or are we that different, some see colors where others see white? The dock light shines into his face.

He lowers the net into the water. The fish scatter, and again, he waits. Eventually they reemerge into the light. He rolls tiny stones into the water; the fish stop abruptly and turn as if spinning on their tails. He grips the net in both hands. One fish tumbles into the net, and he stands rapidly and scoops it up. He swings the heavy net onto the dock. The large fish flip flops under the green diamonds of line.

For a moment he believes he sees sprays of color flying off the fish: blue, green, yellow, red. But, in fact, this is not what he sees at all. He sees bioluminescence, white glowing spots, tiny life in the drops of water coming off the fish's silver body, jumping on the boards of the dock, and falling through the cracks and back into the water. He sees his father's foot stamping the wet sand at night at Juno Beach, sparks flying in all directions. "Look, Willy, look." He sees Jimmy breaking open a sand dollar, collecting the doves, and tossing them into the air. "Look, Daddy, look."

Void of Course

I drag the suitcase through the rainy street, cursing and muttering. It scratches and thumps on the pavement because one of the back wheels is busted. Henry's carrying a laundry bag over his shoulder, and it's got a lot more crap in it than the suitcase. I always pack too much when I visit home, but Henry, he hasn't complained once. This is one night I'm sure glad he's around. I wouldn't have wanted to leave home alone, wouldn't have wanted to be here by myself, on this rainy Seattle street, between the projects and downtown, cars spraying puddles onto sidewalks, old men screaming at themselves and junkies screaming at each other.

The rain comes down steadily. Is there a moon at all? Maybe my sister could have warned me about this night, too. She would have come up with some far-out reason why I just should have kept my mouth shut. Of course, I probably wouldn't have listened—I'd never listened before. So I wonder now why I keep expecting the faces of women on buses to be her face. Why I expect her deep voice to call to me from across an empty room. I expect her to find me in the street. "Angie," she'd say, "what are you doing?"

Henry says, "Let's ride the bus."

"Why?" I ask. "We can't go back to campus. The dorms are locked."

"Because it's dry."

"And get dropped off in fucking nowhere?" If I'd been alone, I would have been crying. When you leave Thanksgiving dinner unfinished before your parents have the opportunity to kick you out, that's what you do. You walk in the rain and cry. But if you have a soft boyfriend with you, a guy who's been there whether you wanted him or not, then you're mean. You can't help it. You attack.

"We don't have to get off," Henry says. "We could just ride the bus all night."

I stop, put the suitcase upright in the road, take my sore hand out of the loop handle, and shake it. "I didn't know you could do that," I say. Rain runs down my neck, under the collar of my jacket—no hood.

"I don't know why you couldn't," Henry says.

"You done it before?"

"Well, no." Henry rests his laundry bag on the curb. Water rolls down the sidewalk and separates on either side of the bag.

"You're getting everything wet." I regret saying this immediately. After all, I've just learned the wrong words could have bigger consequences than you might expect. "Sorry," I say.

I read a poem about that. I was seeing this older guy at the time, and I sent it to him. It was about being careful what you say because, whoever the wise poet was, he said, "The darkness around us is deep." That I remember. Don't mince your words. It's too important. He also said something about elephants in a row, but I can't remember how that fits anymore. Anyway, I sent it to Graham, this man, because I thought he wasn't being so careful with his words, and because some nights I'd feel that darkness pressing in on us.

I look over at Henry, wet dark hair falling around his thin face and resting on his shoulders. That summer the darkness ate Graham and me. But I guess the poem got through to him because I finally got the real words. We were in that dreary motel room, the bed still undone and smelling of sex and sweat, the dark green paisley curtains drawn. The air conditioner rattled in the semi-dark. "I don't love you," he'd said, looking into my face which I knew to be expectant and hopeful.

"Anyway," Henry says, "we could at least find a dry bus stop." I lift the suitcase up over the curb, and Henry leans forward and slings the laundry bag over his shoulder. Henry used to sling fish during the summers, and now he's got a bad back. His legs are planted solidly on the rainy sidewalk.

The one remaining suitcase wheel spins sideways in the sidewalk cracks, and I curse as I pull it along. "Not so fast, Henry."

A large woman with a bloated face is leaning against a wall with a crushed cigarette in her fingers. "Light?" she says. A broken stream of water falls from the eaves and runs down her shoulder. "Sorry," I say. But I dig a dollar out of my pocket. It rattles in the wind. In her eyes are small round white street lights. "Go on," she says after she's taken my dollar. "Go on, now."

The lights of the city reflected against the dark clouds glow a pale yellow. I imagine myself standing outside my parents' dining room, the window with its muted firelight, a pale yellow square. My parents' house is warm. My mother has a plate of pumpkin pie in front of her. My father is swishing cognac. My seat is empty, the chair pulled out from under the table, askew. My napkin on the plate soaks up cranberry sauce. Henry's plate is on the kitchen counter beside the sink which is filled with dirty pots and pans.

I'd said the wrong thing. I said too much. I did not mean this to happen. Sometimes an insult doesn't sound like an insult until it hangs in the air, above a quiet table, on a rainy night. An insult is an insult when the forks stop clicking against the plates. And then there's no turning back.

"What did you say?" my father said.

I couldn't speak, not a word. Henry even was staring at me. "Please speak," his quiet eyes said. "Please make this right." I was struck with shyness, with this shifting inside. It is a matter, my dear, of knowing what we know, but knowing it harder. Some poet again, though I don't think that's exactly how it goes. At this moment, I knew nothing. My mother began to weep. She dropped her face on the white table cloth and wept. We all heard.

"I . . ." I tried.

Henry touched my knee. I looked into his face, his solid, dark eyes, his sturdy gaze.

"We," I reached for his hand under the table, "we have to leave now." It was not what I had wanted to say.

Henry has stopped mid-block and is waiting for me. A woman in a halter top with a distended stomach walks past me jiggling. I watch her thin, bruised legs covered in goose pimples moving like a puppet whose puppeteer can't quite get it right. The first e in Beer hangs upside down on a convenience store marquis. Its windows are barred and the red open sign is turned off.

My sister would have forgiven me for what I'd said tonight. And that's maddening. Because I don't deserve to be forgiven. But Margie, for all her problems, never held anything against anyone. I have to give her that.

Margie was first hospitalized when I was twelve—the crowning incident was the night she left a high school dance and walked all night in the rain. When she came home the next morning, she claimed she'd found a dead child on the beach, but the nearest beach was 40 miles away, and there were no reports of dead children. Saturn, dragging the sun, she said, had led her to Neptune's little secret. When she returned from the hospital a week later, her face vacant and distant, I was filled with rage. She was wearing jeans and a Mexican T-shirt with embroidered flowers. She was still thin, and to anyone else she probably looked like a hip teenager, her straight hair falling halfway down her back, her face distracted just enough to be attractive and mysterious. But to me she was the crazy girl who'd walked in a soaked white dress past all the houses of our neighborhood, block after block after block. She opened her arms to hug me. Behind me I knew my mother was smiling like a doll, smiling like nothing was wrong. She'd spent the morning baking ginger squares for Margie, as if she'd returned from getting a cast put on or getting a tooth pulled. Fury made me dizzy, it made black spots jump in front of my eyes, it made my legs weak.

"Don't touch me!" I shrieked and ran into my bedroom and slammed the door.

Hours later, Margie knocked and I let her in. My face felt swollen from crying. She handed me a cigarette, and we crawled out on the roof and smoked. I'd never had one before. It was all she had to offer. "You can't catch it, you know," she said. And then we fell silent, the balls of our feet pressed against the slanted, tarry shingles, and we watched boys ride bicycles down the street.

The bus stop is at the end of the block. If I caught up to Henry, I'd ask him why the hell he wasn't there keeping my shit dry. Thankfully, I'm back here, moving slowly through the rain, thinking about my sister, seeing her face in the faces of the homeless, in the windows of empty buildings. When you look into someone's face, and they seem to look right through you, are they seeing everything or nothing? Is it self-absorption or empathy? An old man is walking down the street shaking his fist at the night. To me it's not okay to blame God—who I don't believe in anyway—or some phase of the moon for your own issues. You should be held accountable, shouldn't you?

My sister said, "Angie, the moon is void of course." It was June of the summer before last.

"What?" I said. Behind her was a drawing of a bucket of blood with a moon and a black bat.

"Void of course, moving from one constellation to another, and in the meantime, nowhere." Out her bedroom window, I could see the moon with one thin cloud crossing it. It was not nowhere to me. It was hanging in the sky. Perhaps it was my sister who was nowhere, her large face flushed with red splotches, her upper arms huge and limp in her yellow button-up shirt she'd torn the sleeves off of. She was sitting cross-legged on her bed. The blanket was on the ground, and the sheets were disheveled and covered with a thin layer of yellow pollen. She'd insisted on keeping her bed below the window and the screen off, even though occasionally birds flew in, around and out. Some nights she'd screamed.

"Oh," I said and looked skeptically into her big, slack face. Her eyes were shadowed and distant. I saw only what I saw every time I looked at her those last three months, those hot summer months, an impending fall, a fall like the fall of a drunk, his brain soaked in gin, who chokes on his last breath, the fall of an addict whose body shakes until it is forever still. The last sigh, the final spiral, the bottom of a murky ocean. The melted wax of Icarus' fragile wings.

"You don't believe me. Look it up."

I didn't believe her. Not until recently when a girl at school who always wears black gave a report on the phases of the moon and talked about void of course. But by then it was too late, and anyway, it still didn't mean I bought in—that I believed the phase, or in this case the lack of a phase, of the moon was an excuse for someone's actions.

"You have to watch what you say. Move carefully. Don't put yourself in any risky situations," she'd said that night. "Eventually, it will pass."

I think I will never reach the bus stop. Everything in the suitcase must be wet because it feels heavier each moment. I catch up to Henry and we walk side by side, not speaking, not looking at each other. I'm thinking about my mother carrying the platter of turkey out to the table. She's smiling. The room smells of mashed potatoes and meat, and candlelight flickers in the windows. It is as if nothing is missing, as if the pond ice broke and swallowed my sister, but the water froze right over it. Even my father seems no different than he did last Thanksgiving or the Thanksgiving before that. He puts the dark meat aside for me. "This leg's a fat one," he says and gives me his crooked, small smile. He's wearing the red chamois Mom gave him for Christmas last year—in every way, he's the gentle, appropriately festive father. The sound of the rain and the sound of the traffic merge. Rain hangs off my eyelids, and everything looks blurry.

When I was six, my sister took me with her when she broke into a church. "I'll crawl in and then open the door for you," she said as we ducked in the bushes below a window, waiting for the headlights of a car to pass.

I watched her jeans and bare feet disappear beyond the window ledge and waited, pressed against the church's stone wall. I counted to ten. Then I counted to ten again and again and again until the headlights of a car explored the wall, and I ducked into the bushes, my heart shifting and jumping inside me. I counted faster and faster. I counted cars by their headlights, I counted branches in the prickly bush surrounding me. The dirt was cold and wet on my bare legs. "Margie," I whispered loudly, "Margie?" I could hear my own voice trembling. I put my thumb in my mouth and cried.

I don't know how long I lay there, curled up, smelling the dirt, violently sucking my thumb and choking on my tears—an hour? two?—I knew it was too long. When she finally appeared from around the side of the building, her face was red and glistening, and she was wiping her nose with her sleeve. I leapt at her like a bear cub and grabbed her neck and wrapped my legs around her body and wept into her shoulder. I smelled cigarette smoke and sweat. I hated her and I loved her, and I knew that. I was six, and I knew that.

Henry looks at me earnestly from the other side of the plexi-glass of the bus stop. Oh, God. Rain drips down the side of my face. I try unsuccessfully to blow hair out of my eyes. Now he's feeling the bottom of the laundry bag to check how wet it is. Henry is not 40 years old, and he's not married. He doesn't hold my face in his big hands examining me as if I were a child. He doesn't have big hands. He doesn't own a house or even a car. He doesn't rent motel rooms in the middle of the day or call home to check his message machine just after sex.

My sister didn't have lovers—not at the end anyway. How could they have taken the buckets of blood? The Pentel crayons broken and scattered across the floor of her room, ground into the carpets? How could they have taken the constant insistence in her face? Do you love me? Do you love me? The hours of crying. Does God love me? What house is the moon in? The cracks in my palms are too close together. Each obsession a delusion. How could they have dealt with that? They couldn't have.

Henry's my friend. We kiss. We sleep together. We love each other. Henry liked me when we were fifteen, even though the feeling hasn't always been mutual. My father is pouring cognac. He says, "Wish the boy had stayed" and nothing else. Except he touches my mother's arm as she's picking up the gravy dish. She's moving quickly and awkwardly, and the china rattles as she puts it down then leans into the cradle of his arm. His hand rests on her hipbone and he lays his cheek against her back.

"Angie?" I see Henry say, but I can't hear him over the rain ringing around my ears. I stand on the other side of the plexiglass. It doesn't seem right, being on the same side as him.

"Now who's getting things wet?" he says, stepping into the rain. The lights of the bus, like two blinding moons, light his face and hair.

"Fuck you," I say, because there it is. Like, there's my sister breaking the windows of the greenhouse. "There was a man!" she cried. "I had to let him out." Adjusting meds doesn't work if you bury them in the potted plants. I examined the triangles of shattered glass in the grass the next morning. My sister stood behind me with her hands on her big hips. There had been men in her life. I could see their faces in the pieces of glass: Mark who followed her throughout high school. He used to show up at our doorstep in medieval costumes. "Stop calling me your fucking princess!" she hollered one night and threw a pitcher of lemonade across the yard. It sailed through the yellow cone of porch light and fell into the dark, quiet grass. The rock she threw next just grazed Mark's cheekbone. I saw him at the Renaissance Fair a year later, a faint scar running down his face. "Tell Margie I say Hi," he'd said hopefully.

"Fine," Henry says. "Get wet."

I've offended him. So what.

He steps onto the bus. He's cross. I'm cross. The suitcase is impossible to get up the steps. The bus driver glares at me. I can't blame him. Truth is, if you didn't know me, you might think I was homeless too, that I was as crazy as the woman in the tank top jiggling, that I'd flown off some invisible edge. I think of my sister walking in the rain through the neighborhood streetlights in her wet white dress.

Henry lets me have the window seat. Lights blink in and out and through the bus. All I hear is whirring. I don't know where I'm going, but I'm getting wise enough, given the course of the evening, to just keep quiet. I feel Henry's irritation, and I feel like I'm falling, like with Graham in the motel room, the lights from the parking lot turning the curtains yellow, his eyes closed on his middle-aged, businessman's face, touching me and not seeing me, the gray angles at the corners of the window. I wanted to fall then, last summer. Fall away from my sister's diminishing face. I rest my cheek against the window.

"Don't speak," my sister had said. "Shhhh," she said. "Shhhhhhh." She uncrossed her unshaven legs—the bottoms of her feet were black—tucked them under her flowered skirt, and drew her knees into her body as if she were small, which she wasn't. "It's void of course, when communicating goes all wrong."

I looked at the drawing of the bucket of blood hanging on her wall with a tack. My mother called it a candle in the moonlight. But my mother was wrong. I knew better. I knew my sister best. I saw the blood. I saw the bucket. I looked at my sister hugging her knees, the patches of sweat gathering around the rough edges of her shirt's torn armpits. The fan blew dust up from the floor—I watched it spin in summer's evening light. The phone rang.

It was the beginning of the summer, and all I knew of Graham were a couple cups of coffee in a cafe close to school, a suit, a turkey sandwich lunch, and finally a couple beers after school in a bar far out of my neighborhood, far out of his neighborhood, a bar with wood-paneled walls, a low ceiling like in a trailer and sticky tables, with posters of half-naked women emblazoned with beer logos on the bathroom walls and beer signs in every window. It was the bar where I'd scrawled my number on the back of a receipt.

"Don't see him tonight, Angie," she whispered. I wished I hadn't told her anything. "Just wait. It will pass. Everything always does."

I sat in the wooden folding chair, the one piece of furniture my sister brought with her when she returned home the last time. My mother said it looked trashy, but Margie's face pulled so far away, that my mother took it back. "It's lovely," she'd said. "I'm so sorry, Dear." My mother's sunnyness had irritated me. It was as if she'd refused to see. Even my father had talked to Margie like she was a ten-year-old. And this somehow had made my parents complicit.

I put my elbows on my knees, my chin in my palms and listened to my sister. But it was more her voice I heard, and less what she said. It was at once familiar, and then so far away, muted as through a long dark tunnel, a place you wouldn't dare follow.

Hot air blew into my face. Behind Margie, the blue curtains billowed and fell. My hands were sticky. The moment seemed eternal. The phone rang again. I could feel my pulse keeping time. I could feel the dark coolness of the bar and the shock in my body when Graham had wrapped his hand around mine and around the crumpled phone number.

Bodies in sleeping bags are lines under the Yesler Bridge. Henry's right. The bus is warm. The floor heaters are turned on. The bus is mostly empty, and emptiness right now is relief. I push my knees against the seat in front of me, my feet resting on the suitcase. It's Thanksgiving night. I'm on a bus headed nowhere, and my mother, I imagine, is sitting in my sister's room. Clothes and dirt, twigs, leaves, and pollen cover the floor. My mother sits on the dirt and the clothes. She doesn't move a thing. The walls are filled with tacked pictures, ships sinking in red seas, a dead child on the shore, empty houses filled with strips of dusty light, a park bench and a garbage can, a blue temple with a white cross and a bird. A hopeful candle in the moonlight.

My mother sits, and eventually, she leaves. And my father, then he is with her in the wide bed. They may not be speaking, but there they both are, together in the dark.

"Don't answer it," my sister said. Her drawings covered the walls. Dust shifted in the summer light. My sister's arms in her sleeveless, button-up shirt, were blotchy red and glistening. Armpit hair poked out from the torn cloth. I knew my sister was right even though it was hard to look at her face bloated with meds, her newly large and clumsy body bruised from table corners and the edges of doors. The phone rang again, and I left the room.

That night I made love to Graham for the first time. It was like living out your meanest self, like trying to cry louder than your crying sister. I never even knew who he was. The sweat and the elation and the final tears were a roller coaster ride that only brought me closer to the things I feared. I was waving a fist at the sky, I was jiggling and jiggling hoping for stillness. I hated myself. He'd called me, and I had said yes. The moon was gone from the sky as I climbed the motel steps.

I rest my face against Henry's shoulder. Cautiously, he puts his arm around me. At first I'm angered by his shyness. But then I sink lower, my face inside his coat, against his shirt. Thank God. How does meanness help anything? It is nothing more than isolationism and self loathing. At least my mother had held herself together. At least she'd tried to make it easier on all of us.

I'd said the wrong thing. I know my parents didn't lead my sister to her death. I knew it even as I said it. They hadn't denied her illness. As I lean my cheek against Henry's damp and beating chest, I know how they are just like me inside, holding each other in that quiet, dark house after the storm of Thanksgiving dinner has passed. Sometimes there really is no one to blame, not even yourself. I open my eyes cautiously, and look out the window but see only the blurry image of random lights through the glass, now foggy from our breath. I wipe away the steam with my sleeve and search the sky. A full moon is clear in the sky, poised between the lit edges of thick clouds, and I know it has slipped back into its proper course.

The Expense of a View

Lang arrived with flowers. The stems were wrapped in damp paper towel in his fist. When Gracie let him in, he brushed by her, emptied the old flowers into the garbage, and refilled the mason jar he had given her with the fresh ones. How would she tell him?

"New flowers," he said, staring at the ground.

"Thanks." Gracie felt old. She looked beyond him, at her reflection in the dark window, shadowed, ghostlike, tired.

"Is everything alright?" Lang asked.

"Sure, Lang. Everything's okay. You haven't eaten have you? I've had black-eyed peas on all day."

"Black-eyed peas?" he asked.

"Sure, black-eyed peas," Gracie said, pulling two wooden bowls from the cupboard.

"I've never had black-eyed peas." He leaned against the doorway between the kitchen and the living room. Gracie didn't look at him. She knew what he looked like, and she was bored, bored with his clean face and his I've-never-been-anywhere eyes.

"Really?" She opened the drawer beside the sink for two spoons. "Well, I've never cooked them before."

He followed her into the kitchen. "What's in it?" he asked, peering over her shoulder as she dunked a mug with a broken handle into the pot.

"Spinach, hot sausage—real hot, there's beer—garlic and lemon pepper. This woman that lived next door to us when I was a kid used to make them for me. When things got bad, I could always go next door and eat black-eyed peas. I've been meaning to try it for a long time."

"Bad?" Lang said still staring into the pot. "What things got bad?"

"I don't know," she said. There was a sharp pain in her right temple.

"What do you mean you don't know? You just said—"

"I know what I just said. I don't know, Lang. For the life of me, I don't know." For the life of me, perhaps her mother had said that? Perhaps Mrs. Kinny? It sounded wrong in her own mouth. But there was no other way to say about the not knowing.

"Okay," he said. "Don't get uptight."

"I'm not." She closed her eyes slowly. They burned. Her forehead felt tender.

Halfway through the meal Gracie left Lang at the table and lit candles throughout her kitchen. Her head ached. She opened the window above the sink. Towels were bending and twisting on the clothesline above blackberry brambles and the small, weedy garden terraces on the hillside. The towels had been on the line since summer.

"It's raining hard now," she said before she sat down again. The foghorns started up, loud and dull through the dark.

"Lang," she said, her voice filling the painful space around her head. "I'd like to stop this." The bowls were empty. Five empty beer bottles were pushed up against the window sill. Lang stared at the bottles as if counting. The ache moved along the corner of Gracie's forehead and across the top of her face.

"Stop what?"

She glanced briefly at his dark blue eyes, the wave of dusty hair across his forehead.

"I don't want to go halfway on this. I don't think it would be fair." She tried to count the two years she had been here, a year and half of that time with Lang, but it had disappeared without the counting. "Us," she said finally.

"Do you mean you don't want to see me?"

"I don't think I should be seeing you now."

"Excuse me, do I have some say in this?"

"I don't think so."

"Gracie, I—" He stopped. The silence seemed to shatter on the linoleum.

That night Gracie held Lang tightly. Her face felt hot against his back. She dreamed she was a child and all the air was sucked out of her small room, four cardboard walls filled with nothing. She ran into the night in a white T-shirt and underpants screaming, but no sound would come out. When she woke, Lang was holding her tightly. She reached for her breath then lay awake listening to the five o'clock trucks on Marine Drive.

⸺⸺⸺

Gracie worked weekdays, nine to five. She stood all day over the BioProducts counter measuring liquids in beakers, considering the difference between empty and full, marking glass with a black oil pen. At lunch she sat on the rocks by the river with a sandwich. The smell of excess fish parts filled the part of her that had no scent at all.

Once, near the end of the work day, as the windows were turning dark, Gracie became fixated on a spider. She had been staring at her thin face in the glass, the outline of her blonde hair chopped short and large foreign eyes looking back at her from a place she took care not to know, when she saw the spider crawling up the gray window drape. It moved in and out of the folds of cloth like some trickster who appears and disappears behind street lamps after the parade has gone and only paper cups litter the empty street. She dropped a beaker and grabbed at her stomach. Glass spread across the cement floor.

On the weekends she walked along the railroad tracks by the river and into town. On Valentine's Day a man was selling handmade candles out of a van beside the tracks. At the edge of the hardware store parking lot two women were pulling flowers from buckets, one at a time, and arranging them in tissue paper. An entire bucket of blue carnations sat untouched.

On Main Street, a man stood on the corner wearing a pin-striped suit, a red tie, and red shoes. A red handkerchief was folded neatly in his coat pocket. His fingers looped in red suspenders, he was grinning at Gracie who was still a block away, his mouth slack and wide. She had seen him a number of times working at the Rehab Center where she bought secondhand clothes and dishes. He held the string of a balloon in his fist. The balloon was silver and red in the shape of a heart with letters on it. He waited at the corner, ignoring both lights when they turned white. When she reached him, he stepped toward her.

"I'm Stevey." He groped for her hand.

"Hi Stevey." His face was bumpy and blotched, and his nose, too large for his face, looked permanently swollen.

"It's my birthday. I'm forty-three today."

"That's great." He let her hand go, and she turned to leave.

"Read my balloon," he said. She looked up into the too-clear sky. *I love you* wagged stupidly against the glaring light. Stevey laughed, loud and out of place. He couldn't keep it in somehow. Gracie put her head down and walked quickly away.

That night Gracie pulled a brown plaid suitcase from the large closet she had converted into a guest room. She filled it with nothing. The cat sat on the stereo cocking her small head as Gracie left with the suitcase.

When she returned half an hour later, the cat was still on the stereo, and the suitcase was still empty. Edith mewed once, twice, then ran into the kitchen. Gracie filled her empty food dish. When she turned around, Edith was glaring at the water bowl, one wet paw held up. She swatted the bowl just enough to tip it. A small creek trickled across the linoleum. Edith dipped a paw in and stepped back, her head cocked forward.

"Oh Ms. Piaf," Gracie said as she refilled the bowl and placed it back on the linoleum.

———

A week later Gracie, in a peacoat and black watch cap, walked into a bar not a mile from her apartment where a bluegrass band was playing in the corner. She glanced at the band. A blond man with a thin boyish face looked back at her. She headed for the bar. The room was box-shaped with high ceilings and huge windows made up of small square panes which looked out onto the highway. Out back past the parking lot was a red building where ships had once been built, and beyond that, beyond the tracks, was a long dock, half of which had fallen into the river, inaccessible due to a barbed-wire fence. Gracie figured the bar would attract another crowd completely if only the square panes faced the river. But a hundred years ago, view hadn't been the first concern. Besides, who in Uniontown could afford view? Who had ever been able to afford a view?

Gracie sat by the window, now on her third beer, resting her elbow on the wide pane. Voices magnified in the open space and overwhelmed the unamplified players. She watched the banjo player, wondering at his bent face, then staring at his hands as if memorizing the pattern of his fingers. Her body might not have existed. Inside of her was a longing she refused to identify but that had returned over and over throughout her life. It had crawled into her stomach like some parasitical beast.

At the end of the piece, the small blond man looked at Gracie and grinned. His front teeth were missing. Her fingers moved up and down through the sweat on her beer bottle, her face hot and her insides numb. He laid his banjo in its case, purple-lined and battered, grabbed his beer from the window sill and walked towards her.

"You mind if I sit here?"

"Not at all," she murmured.

"I can't hear you," he said. He sat down and leaned across the table thrusting his face at her.

"Not at all," she repeated. "Not at all, I don't mind if you sit here."

"Thanks." He leaned back. "What's your name? You've been in here before."

"Gracie."

"You come in here alone."

She nodded.

"I'm Andy, in case you wanted to know." His arms were crossed over his chest. "Where are you from?"

"Here," she answered, considering the two years she had been here, two years before that she had been somewhere else, before that somewhere else, and always always always from Louisiana. "Where are you from?"

"Mississippi originally. I been here awhile though. I came here to fish. But I lost my ass enough times, too many new rules now to make it worthwhile anymore."

She could have guessed. Gracie had erased the South from her voice. What that left her with she wasn't too sure. She had come here because she had ended up here, because she had run out of gas, out of money, and out of cat food, because the waves of lunacy in this corner of the world matched her own. "How long have you been playing banjo?" Gracie asked.

" 'Bout as long as I can remember. My Daddy played the fiddle. He was always coming and going."

Coming and going, like Edith came and went through the kitchen window, once carrying a starling in her mouth, the screen door slamming, Gracie's bare feet running through the grass, out one door in another, tears falling all over the place, snot on her sleeve. Mrs. Kinny cookin' black-eyed peas again, steam on her bent face.

She tore at the label on the beer bottle.

Andy put his elbows on the table and leaned close to her. "You get stoned?" he whispered. She stared into the black circle between his teeth and nodded. "Let's go," he said finishing off his pale beer. She swallowed down the remaining half a beer, grabbed her hat, and followed him out the door and around the building. Bits of gravel shown white, and beyond she could just make out the barbed-wire fence leading out to the dock. The whole world felt forbidden.

Andy unzipped his jacket, reached below his ragg sweater, torn under the arm, to a chest pocket, and drew out a joint which he readily lit. Thousands of small, bare feet were running inside the grass in her chest, and she was glad for the sedative. She stared numb at the river, which she couldn't see, only the fence. Without failure, she always expected dope to sooth her, to control the grinding of her dark and cold insides. And without failure, dope made her want to throw herself onto the ground where she would then lapse into uncontrollable fits. And, without failure, she refused to exhibit any such behavior and stood motionless and blank, Gracie dead eye.

"Come on Grace," he whispered. A warm hard liquor smell she hadn't noticed before pressed up against the side of her face. "Come on Grace," his mouth against her ear, his hands moving frantically down her back, her butt, the back of her legs, her arms hanging limp, her face soaked and silent.

———⌒⌒⌒———

A week later Gracie let three messages play. She had let them bleep silent red for over a week. They were all from Lang. She sat on her sofa staring past her reflection and out at the rain. How could she possibly see him now? Now when she could hardly even account for herself? She pulled the suitcase out of the closet and filled it with nothing. Ms. Piaf was dipping her paw into spilled water as it made its way to the cracks in the linoleum.

Gracie stood on cement rubble that remained from a cannery that had burnt down not six months before. She squatted in the shadow of the bridge. The sky was gray and darkening. Unnamed fog ghosts wove their way among the coast mountains across the river. None of this was anything she recognized. Nothing reminded her of Louisiana. Still, this baggage.

She held open the empty suitcase over the water and dumped it. Nothing splashed into the sludge. She closed the suitcase and stood. She walked up the path between rocks, past blackberries that threw their dormant arms in her way. On the edge of a parking lot in the grass she stepped to the side to avoid a needle. The traffic on Marine Drive repeated itself over and over again, a waking and a sleeping rumble.

She was standing on the curb watching the cars when Stevey joined her. He stood beside her at first and watched the cars too.

"Hi," he said.

"Hi," Gracie said. She turned to look at him, as if perhaps his disfigured face had become more familiar and comforting to her than anything had been in a long time.

But when she turned to look, out of the depths of her silent body rose a screaming familiarity. The face was battered and scraped. There was a patch over one eye, and below the chin was a deep gouge the size of a large cockroach.

"They beat me up," Stevey said. "Maybe next they'll kill me. They call me names. They tell me about their knives and my ugly face."

She had seen a face so battered. There were no sounds, nothing around her, no traffic on Marine Drive, only the battered face, the battered face, the battered—

"Momma!" Gracie screamed. She stood in the kitchen doorway, her mother's head lifting off the floor, blood across the linoleum and shrieks on her mother's cracked face. Poppa's big hands, Gracie touching the wall with her fingers, Momma saying, "Go, go, you go." Go, she goed, out the door she goed, through the grass she goed and goed and goed.

Stevey put his hand on her shoulder. "You're my friend, aren't you?" he said.

"Yes," she said. "Yes." All of it came back, the traffic, each car and its own noise on the road, a car that rattled below, a truck that groaned deep, a high whirring from somebody. She saw that she could cross the street. "You take care," she said to the face. "Please take care." She ran and was pushed across Marine Drive and into a world of things she had forgotten.

The key shook in her hand. Her stomach was alive and furious. She dropped the suitcase and walked around the entire apartment, once, twice, again, then again, opening doors, shutting doors, the face was in the extra bedroom, on the kitchen floor, everywhere the face.

Someone knocked on the door. Lang.

"Come in," she said. She was standing against the wall with both her two hands held against her own face. The empty suitcase lay open in the center of the living room floor.

"Are you alright?" he asked immediately. She studied his face, moments and more, his face seeing hers, his softness disturbed, and the disturbed in her softening. There were no flowers.

Three of Swords

An old man abducted a small child. She was four. I'm certain she was four. I saw it happen. He picked her up off the sidewalk and put her under his arm. She cried the whole time, but he called her by a name that wasn't her name so no one would know he was a stranger. But I knew. He took her to his house with broken windows and black mold spreading across the walls. There was a TV and a mattress with stuffing coming out of it and a La-Z-Boy chair that would never return to its upright position.

I know this because I see things other people can't see. For example, I dreamed Jenny's cats were gathered together in the barn, but Sebastian was missing. When the cats turned toward me, their eyes had human lashes and human tears, and I knew Sebastian was dead. Sebastian was gone the next morning, and a week later, a neighbor said she'd found him dead in an alley, his eyes bulging out of his gray and white whiskered face. She said he looked "Oddly human."

I saw the abduction when I was walking to the corner store for cat food. It was hot and white out and the street smelled like garbage. I knew the man was abducting the girl when I saw him lift her off the sidewalk. I knew because I was abducted too. Jenny abducted me. Now she makes me see for her. She asks me to read the cards, like I did the day I predicted Lawrence would go to jail. Lawrence is a mandolin player who comes to open mics Jenny has in her barn. He was in AA, but then he went off the wagon. He threatened to burn down the neighborhood off south Martin Luther King. And I saw it, saw him standing behind the wands in the cards, saw him trapped, saw the devil card that was him going off the wagon. I said, "I think that's Lawrence." And then Jenny and I didn't say anything, both of us staring at the cards, wondering what Lawrence was doing there.

Jenny crawled in my window one night when my parents were sleeping. She covered my mouth with her hand and bound my wrists behind my back with a strip of white sheet. Then she put another strip across my mouth and tied it around my head. I tried to scream, but the sheet crossed under my tongue, and my tongue was pressed up against the roof of my mouth. I breathed heavily through my nose and moaned deep in my throat, but my parents kept sleeping. I imagined them holding each other, my father breathing against my mother's neck; I imagined them dreaming of a picnic—the three of us beside a lake with bright green hills sloping off into the distance and small white bunnies chasing each other along the shore and wild horses galloping into the horizon. In the dream, we're sitting on a checkered blanket, me in between the two of them, watching the bunnies play. I wished Jenny'd let me scream. I know they would've woken up. I know it.

Instead, she forced me downstairs through the kitchen, where a bag of garbage sat in the center of the floor, and the cupboards were half opened. On the counter was an empty carton of Capri Menthol Lights. One cupboard was empty except for a canister of my mother's Slimfast. And my mother's round face, thick red hair falling over blue eyes—red rimmed, puffy eyes, delicate as a child's—rose before me. I looked so different, sometimes I wondered if I'd ever been part of her. When I was little, she'd pull me into her arms, rest her head on top of mine and hug me. She'd buy me candy bracelets and clip-on earrings and sparkly lipstick whenever I was sick or upset or sometimes just because.

I tried to grab the door so Jenny couldn't close it. Jenny's not very big, but she's very strong in her body and in the way she can talk people into doing things they don't want to do. She dragged me through my neighborhood, pulling me by my elbow through the shadows, avoiding the direct light of street lamps. People were arguing. I could hear them hitting one another and screaming. A man and a woman. I faced away from Jenny and watched my house, and the screaming and weeping seemed to rise up out of it. But I knew that wasn't true. The screaming rose up out of the ground, rose up from the sewers as if the neighborhood itself were screaming, not my crooked house where my parents lay holding each other and dreaming of me. And then we were running, Jenny with her black magic forcing me to run, the screaming growing fainter and fainter and fainter still. Garbage shone white in the moonlight and broken glass littered the gray road.

Jenny took me here, to this small, hidden pocket of country in the city, to this barn and this house guarded by punk trees smelling like rotting paper in the humid night, just like the man took the girl to his house. I know where the man took the girl.

After I saw him take her, I went to the corner store with bars on its windows. I saw my face between the bars, thin and distant and pale, distraught from seeing. I saw no one I recognized in my dark eyes and limp hair. My body looked small in the space between the bars. Then I saw the girl's face looking back at me; she was crying. Her jaw was streaked with a thin line of dirt, and her hair frizzed about her eyes. On the sidewalk outside the store was a used condom.

Inside, hotdogs spun in a glass box, and there was a display of jalapeno poppers, old fried chicken pieces, fried catfish, and barbeque sandwiches. The air smelled of grease, and for a moment

I stopped and leaned my hand against a soda pop cooler to keep from vomiting. I imagined my stomach a shriveled, empty sack. The abducted girl will not eat.

I stumbled through the heat with the bag of cat food cans as if I were lost seeing everything inside me instead of everything outside, the station wagon he took her in, the crooked house he took her to, the boarded windows, the screaming neighborhood. In the distance, two ragged boys were pushing a shopping cart full of mangos and shouting out for customers. My legs were sweating under my long black skirt, and they felt weak from the walking. White spots jumped around the edges of my vision, sunflakes, and as I walked, each footfall was like a little hammer against the back of my head, crawling up my scalp and embedding itself into my forehead. I kept my eyes open just enough to see.

I crossed a highway and cut through a parking lot. Old Florida houses were hidden in brush. I stepped around fallen grapefruit split open on the sidewalk. The highway, which separated me from the rest of the city—the corner store and Martin Luther King— echoed in the otherwise silent heat. The green and the shade made me feel a little less like fainting, and the spots in my eyes went away. I walked past two men drinking beer on a couch on a porch and shifted the bag in my arms because one arm felt dead. I thought of my father and his friends, hours on the front porch, their voices ringing in night. One day when I was a child, I saw a man's back walking down the street, right down the middle of the road, getting farther and farther away. Sometimes I don't under-stand what I see until it happens. Often I see things and record them in my mind and then I wait. I stared into the green branches of trees and listened to my feet's quiet connection with the cement as if I were walking through a dream tunnel of green shade.

I stumbled back to Jenny's house and Jenny's barn, hidden like many of the houses around here, a headache in the corner of my forehead from all the seeing. I left the cans on the kitchen counter. Jenny wasn't home. The kitchen smelled of cat food; empties were loaded into a paper bag on the corner, their jagged tops still coated with food. The house smelled of old incense and patchouli oil, and somehow the mix of the incense and the cat food and the kitty litter was worse than the cat food and the kitty litter alone would have been. A black tomcat rubbed up against my leg, his tail high in the air.

"Go away," I said.

He mewed and rubbed again.

I pushed him with my toe. "Go away."

He complained again and dug his claws into the leg of the kitchen table. I stood still in the hot kitchen listening to the scratching; it felt like the scratching inside me.

I went into the barn and dug my cards out of the horse trough. They were covered with hay. There aren't any cows, but there is hay. There was a horse, but she's dead now. Her name was Nocturne. I used to imagine Jenny riding her through the city streets late at night, Jenny's black hair flying behind her. Nocturne was gray and black and white, marbled like a tortoiseshell cat, and she had one blue eye and one black eye. Jenny got her from a children's riding barn because she was wild. When I first started coming to the open mics in Jenny's barn, she still had the horse, and at the breaks between sets I'd lean against the pasture's fence and listen to Nocturne snorting in the dark. Behind me the other musicians and writers smoked and talked and drank coffee. One night Nocturne came near me; I didn't reach out my hand because I didn't want to scare her. She arched her neck and lowered her nose and stood beside the fence looking at me with her one blue eye, breathing heavily into the night, her body so still she seemed frozen. That was before Jenny knew about my seeing, when she was still just the crazy cat woman who ran the music and poetry nights in the barn, and I was only the silent girl in black who sat in the shadows.

Jenny likes to touch my cards, so I have to hide them. It's not right that she should play with them. She has no respect. I brushed bits of hay off the wrapped cards and tucked them under the elastic of my skirt. I lit a black candle in a wrought iron candle holder that hung on the wall. The holder swung a little, hit the wall, and stopped. I lit another tall, silver candle in a candle holder with a handle and brought it with me to the center of the floor where I wiped aside the hay and brushed at the dirt, careful not to get a splinter up my fingernail. I unwrapped the cards from their worn silk bandana.

My hands were pale, my nails bitten short and painted black like little dark moons. I concentrated hard on my hands, everything that could course through them. I concentrated so hard I could not feel my hands at all. I could not feel myself at all. There is so little of me to feel. The barn walls turned gray and undefined with blurry lights from which energy hummed. I laid out the cards. The little girl was the Page of Cups, and the old man was the Magician.

Five of Swords. In his insecurity he stole from ragged people. He collected her from a battlefield after the battle. South Martin Luther King Street. The corner store with bars on the windows. Boys with guns. Empty Styrofoam food containers. Piles of soggy clothes in bushes. Used condoms. Angry voices.

Six of Swords. They rowed in a boat together. That would be the street. He rowed, and she sat huddled in a cloak, crying. He took her to an island; that would be his house.

Three of Swords. A heart pierced with three knives. She's separated from her parents. They are not smart people. They are poor and busy and they argue a lot. She often plays alone. She should not have been on the street alone. It's not their fault. She misses them very much. Each moment the distance is greater. Her heart is bleeding.

Seven of Swords. She's bound and blindfolded with strips of sheet. There are pools of rain water all around her. The rain water has come in from the broken windows. She can smell the mold. Even the mattress is damp. The TV is on. People are arguing on a soap opera, but she does not know it is the TV. It sounds like home. Her bleeding heart aches.

Nine of Wands. He keeps her head lower than the windows so no one can see in. He stands at the door and looks out. He paces. He turns down the TV at the commercial so he can listen for intruders. Giant white wands the size of trees surround the house.

Five of Cups. He looks out the window. Behind him he's spilled three cups of red wine on the carpet. There are still two full cups, but he does not see them. He looks out the window and for a moment, regrets.

Death. Jenny says this card means change. But what does she know? I think it is simpler than that. The child will die here.

—◊—

Jenny shakes my shoulder.

"Christine," she says. "You'll burn down the barn one of the these days." My face is in the hay, and I'm curled on my side. My skirt covers my ankles. I feel small in my black clothes. Jenny is holding a Budweiser. She's kneeling beside me, her long black hair covering much of her face. Gray hairs poke through her dye job. A tabby cat moves around her feet and rubs against her hip purring. Even in the dark, I can see the wrinkles around her eyes. The mole beside her eyebrow casts a tiny shadow. She strokes my arm, but my arm doesn't feel it. My arm is floating away. My body is sleeping still.

"A girl was abducted today," I say.

"Have you eaten?" she asks.

I don't answer.

"Come on, Christine." She grips my arm and lifts me up. I know she's bruising me. I follow her out of the barn. The shaggy white punk trees rustle and stink in the hot breeze. It's almost dark, and I walk slowly with my head down. I've collected my cards and have tucked them under the elastic band of my skirt. They burn against my hipbone.

Inside the house is too bright. It stinks of cats. The ceiling fan is on, but it's only pushing around the hot air that occasionally comes in through the screens. I stand in the doorway, close my eyes, and listen to the whir of the fan. There is a ceiling fan in the house where the girl is. It whirs behind the sound of the TV. Like any good prisoner, the girl will refuse to eat. I turn off the wall light and open my eyes to the new dimness. Jenny is lighting candles and incense. On the top of a low bookshelf, flames spark off Jenny's crystals. She's made black-eyed peas and rice while I've been asleep in the barn. I'm surprised I didn't hear her drive up. She fills my plate, and I stare into it. But my stomach doesn't want it, and neither do I. Still, I put a bite in my mouth, just to make a show of it, but I don't eat it. It dissolves on my tongue. Jenny lights a pipe, and we smoke. I drink her beer.

A cat jumps up on the corner of the table, and I push it off. It mews in protest and jumps up again.

"Go away," I say and shove it off again.

It jumps into Jenny's lap, and she lets it stay there, its face peering over the edge of the table, its yellow eyes glaring at me.

"You should eat something," Jenny says.

"I did," I say.

"You're white as a ghost."

"I am a ghost." The Magician offers the Page of Cups a piece of white bread, but she doesn't eat. She's empty inside.

Jenny stands up, and the cat leaps across the room. She stands behind me and rubs my back, but my back doesn't feel it. I imagine round blue-gray fingerprints on my shoulders where she squeezes. She's a witch, and she's pressing spells into my bones.

"Did the smoke help settle your stomach?"

I nod, but this is a lie. I feel like sliding onto the floor and sleeping, but I know the carpet stinks. The thought of if it makes me want to vomit, though there's nothing in my stomach to get rid of except for a few sips of Jenny's beer.

"Do you want to practice?" she asks.

I want to get out of the house, away from the smell of the cats and of bacon, away from the plate of beans. "I have a new song," I say, although I don't quite know what it is yet.

I stand up and lean against the wall, watching Jenny blow out the candles. All I hear is the little poof of her breath, again, again, again. A coolness creeps through my head as the darkness takes over the house, and as I slowly blink my eyes, the headache falls away, and the floaty feeling from the dope and beer take over. Jenny goes into her room to get her bass. A gray cat stands with one foot in my food eating. I listen to the lap lap lap of its coarse tongue.

Jenny stands in the doorway to her room holding my guitar and her bass. "Would you like to play?"

"I just want to sing."

"You sure?" she asks.

Lap, lap, lap. "Get off!" I shove at the cat with my hand.

I follow Jenny back out to the barn. This time she turns on the lights. Dust floats in layers, each speck a life abandoned.

Jenny sets up the speakers and plugs in her bass. The child's face is floating in my mind, her wet eyes, her little body like a bundle of brittle twigs under the Magician's strong, withered arm. Jenny stands on the stage she built and plays a few notes. They're off key. Jenny likes things off key. She kicks at the hay with her cowboy boots. I sit on the edge of the stage. I won't let her look at me. Jenny plays her three chords and I stare into the rafters where a bit of twine thick with dust, like a line in the water gets thick with seaweed, hangs. Nocturne's old bridle hangs from the wall, and somewhere in Jenny's primitive, discordant playing, I imagine Nocturne's wild blue eye, and I wonder about freedom and death, captivity and life.

I am singing before I realize I've begun. My voice separates from my body. It is quiet and not exactly singing. It's more like humming, like moaning and whispering. There are words, but they, like Jenny's chords, don't fit together. I make them up as I go along, and as I go along, I can hear all the sounds coming together, like a body gathering up its parts: the sounds of the highway whirring far in the background, Jenny's discordance, a whippoorwill outside the barn, the day's small sounds—Jenny blowing out the candles, cats lapping food and scratching wood, boys selling mangos. These sounds momentarily push away the others that seem to always be with me—the screaming, the weeping. I remember feeling this way at the open mics, sitting in the darkness listening to music, one person after another, how everything else disappeared, even myself. Even when the AA-ers sang "Amazing Grace," even then, I let it wash through me—at the end of those evenings when the others had left, I'd help Jenny clean up, and she'd make jokes about how much coffee the AA-ers had gone through. It got so each day at school, when I used to go, I thought about the next open mic, even though they only happened once a month. Maybe that's when I started coming even when there was no open mic. But that was all before Jenny knew about my seeing.

A yellow cat stands in the door and swats at the dust. I hum and my hum mingles with the hot night air thick with humidity. We stop together. Jenny puts her bass down and sits beside me. "That was lovely," she says. She kisses my cheek as if she's proud of me. Then she says, "Why don't you go back to school, Christine?"

"I want to be a singer," I say. "You told me we could be a band together." My throat constricts. It's dry and tight and I want Jenny to be quiet. I want the floaty feeling back. But now there's a sharpness in my throat, and my stomach clenches like a rock. I don't even know how long it's been since I've been to school, or how long I've been here.

"I can still teach you guitar," she says. "You can still sing."

The buzz of crickets covers the sound of the city as best it can. The streets have an infuriating hum. I used to hold my hands over my ears when I couldn't stand it any longer. I swallow, but the ache in my throat only tightens.

"You can still stay here," Jenny says. "You'll always have a place to stay. No one will turn you away again."

Tears build up behind my eyes. I try hard not to feel my face, but it's hot. Jenny's arm is around my shoulder. I see the little man moving farther and farther away.

The Magician tries to make the Page of Cups comfortable. He lets her rest on the La-Z-Boy. But the La-Z-Boy is damp. He tries.

"You're so smart," Jenny says. "I was never that smart."

I wipe the arm of my sweater across my face. I think about the guitar Jenny gave me, about Jenny pressing my fingers against the strings, teaching me chords. How I'd spend hours after school in her barn, my fingers sore and bleeding, waiting for her to come home from work. I could never quite get it right, but I liked the way I could put little bits of myself into each note and let them drift away.

"A girl was abducted today," I say weakly staring at blurry bits of hay scattered across the warped floorboards.

"No, Christine. Please."

"I saw. The Magician—"

"I just don't understand," she says. "You see so much— Sebastian's death, Lawrence going to jail, but you can't see yourself."

There is an exhaustion in her voice and a slow, stammering persistence. The smell of gardenias drifts into the barn. Just outside the door are three white blossoms. "You could write a book about all our futures. But Christine, you were not abducted."

I look into Jenny's face, strong in its own way, and for a brief moment, my mind registers her concern. For a moment I don't see the witch or the abductress, and I can hardly believe she's put up with me. One day I came home from school and I knew that my parents had left for good. And there was only one place left to go.

Jenny and I stood in my parents' kitchen, Jenny carrying a laundry bag of my clothes, and me holding a box of photos and old plastic toys and books. It's all I had. The cupboards were empty except for my mother's Slimfast, and the house was silent, silent of their fighting, silent of my father and his friends drinking, silent of the constant murmur of the TV, silent of my mother's weeks of crying after my father had left. I stared at the water stains on the kitchen's ceiling and at the boarded window and felt myself drifting away. I imagine a man walking down the middle of the road, his back getting smaller and smaller. I imagine my mother in someone else's crappy kitchen standing over a gas burner shaking a spoon.

It all feels like somebody else's story, and I'm scared. Scared of what else I can't see—a little me balancing on a pinnacle between clarity and emotion's warping of intuition. I imagine Nocturne running circles around the pasture, pawing at the dust, snorting and rearing and bucking and fighting to live. I rest my face against Jenny's shoulder and cry.

Thinking About Carson

My dog and I love the ocean. Daily, we wander up and down the coast. Today, like many days, we walked in the rain. Clean spray fell diagonally into my face and rested on my cheeks and nose and lips. Martin wandered up against the dunes weaving his way among the driftwood pieces, pushing kelp around with his nose, chewing on fish bones and old bird wings. I walked as close to the receding ocean as possible. Tillamook Head was obscured in gray, and that gray reflected itself in wide tidal flats. Water pooled around the soles of my boots. I like walking in those reflected areas; the world is solid and repetitive, wide and silent.

Before Oregon, the world was broken up into pieces. Landscapes were broken up into streets and buildings and windows and doors and cars and faces; people were broken apart by words and hands and boots and objects sailing wickedly through the air. Imagine a spare and clean kitchen floor covered with broken glass. Imagine a quiet night, white curtains billowed with a steady wind. You are a child dreaming peacefully. You are woken by unremitting screams, the screams of someone else's nightmare where the breaking down process is no longer variable but constant.

Martin and I moved here three years ago. Our life is quiet now. We live in a little apartment in a small town of colored houses. Everywhere there is a view of the mouth of the Columbia River. It rains all winter, and the street signs and railway posts turn green with lichen and moss. The sound of the rain helps me sleep at night.

I find I think of Carson often. She's been gone six months now, and I think of her more each day instead of less. She's with me at the beach only she's barefoot, and she's wading through the pools. Rain sticks to the soft whitish hair that grows in a cowlick from the corner of her forehead. She's holding her shoes, and her pants, although rolled halfway up her calves, are wet. Carson once told me she used to believe it was three miles to the horizon. But the trick was, she said, no matter how far out you swam, it was still three miles. Three miles away, gray meets gray. I whistle to Martin, and the two of us turn back toward the trail through the dunes.

When we return from the beach, there's a postcard from Carson waiting in the mailbox. The postcard is from Mexico. It's of an empty beach, although she claims she has yet to see one empty. The postcard's addressed to "a boy and his dog." On the back Carson's drawn pictures of the different shells she's found, a cat's eye, a king's crown, a whelk. Her drawings are childish and utterly charming. She writes she ate a coconut she found on the street. She met a dog who shared it with her. She misses Martin. She misses me.

Martin settles himself under the kitchen table. His toenails click on the linoleum. I know he's resting his nose across his front paws. I think of Carson the most in the mornings. I used to wake with my nose against the back of her neck. My arm would be draped over her, and her arm would be draped over Martin who'd be lying on the floor beside the mattress.

Carson liked to sleep late, but I've always gotten up early. From beneath Carson's arm, Martin would open his old eyes and look at me like I was crazy for leaving her each morning then slowly close them again. I'd shower and sometimes sweep or mop or dust; then, I'd sit in the kitchen with my coffee. Eventually I would wake Carson. I'd lie on top of her and press my face into her ear. She was always happy to see me in the mornings. But the nights were a different thing.

—⟋⟍⟍—

The first time it happened, I was dreaming of Alaska. The sun was the moon. It was night but everything was lighted. The snow was a pale blue color. I was in a tiny boat surrounded by icebergs. Carson screamed. The ice broke apart, cracking as loud as guns, and blue shards of it tore my little sail lengthwise and in half. As I opened my eyes, Carson was leaping out of bed, and not until she reached the door, did she turn back to look at me. I watched as the wall broke up into a door and the shape of a naked woman. I couldn't speak. She stood with one hand on the door frame, her mouth partway open as if she were deciding whether or not she would scream again. She looked over her shoulder into the darkened living room, then back at me, at the walls, at the window, the gray light pressed up against the other side of the blinds. Finally she came back and sat on the edge of the bed.

I reached over and rubbed her arm and she crawled into bed and curled up beside me. I stroked her hair, and she pressed her face into my shoulder. I stared at the ceiling trying to make it stay one solid piece, but it kept breaking apart into jagged fragments pushing up against one another. It was like looking at a window that had broken and was trying to fix itself, but the pieces of glass didn't fit anymore. They just kept breaking down.

—⟋⟍⟍—

I pull spinach, garlic, a carrot, and an egg out of the refrigerator. The house still smells of the beach and of whatever dead thing Martin rubbed into the side of his neck, even though I've sprayed him off with the hose and sprayed the apartment with an air freshener; Carson always hated that stuff. She wouldn't have noticed the smell at all, or she would have said, "It's part of Martin, how can you not love that?" I do my best to ignore it, hoping in some way to change an outcome that has already passed. Still, I end up cracking open the window above the sink no more than two inches. A dark breeze fills the kitchen.

I wash my hands and wash the vegetables and chop them into small bits then mix in the egg. All this I pour on a bowl of dry dog food for Martin. He sits beside me watching. I worry that Martin is old. I want him to go on living longer than me, but I know that's not likely. I've dreamed of him flying out of windows, and when I wake I stalk the house looking for him. Sometimes he's beside my mattress. Sometimes he's sleeping under the kitchen table or under my desk. Sometimes, although rarely, he's on the blanket I've designated as his. When I find him, I wake him to make sure he's breathing. "Martin," I say. "Martin, you alive?" It's happened more often since Carson's been gone.

The smell of seaweed and of something dead still lingers. I vacuum my bedroom and the living room. I pull the cushions off the sofa and vacuum there also. I boil water for pasta and pour myself a glass of wine. A sausage is thawing in the refrigerator. I flip through the newspaper and stare out at the rain.

—— ᗯᗯ ——

The second time it happened, Carson discovered me staring at the ceiling. Her scream had been long and loud and shrill, and it wavered the way two notes waver when they meet in tune then turn sharply away. Afterwards, I thought she'd fallen asleep with her face on my shoulder, but as it turned out, she'd been watching me. My eyes were glossy with tears, and I was staring at the ceiling watching a little house made of glass cubes tumble through the air.

"Myer," she said.

"Huh?"

"Are you okay?"

One box gave way, and the others began to topple down, at first making a soft shuffling sound, and gradually building to a shattering pitch and echoing deep inside my ear.

"I'm so sorry," she said, touching my forehead and stroking my hair. "I didn't mean to frighten you."

The rain pounded against the window. My heart thumped rapidly inside me. "My mother used to scream in her sleep," I said finally. Carson kissed my cheek and around my eyes. I could feel regret in her kisses. Her childhood had been as violent as mine, and now here it was, in bed with me. I had deceived myself. I hadn't escaped at all. How could I let my life be broken apart like this again?

The water boils. I wash my hands again and pull pasta out of a glass container where it stays fresh from moisture and bugs. Then I put the sausage in a frying pan with a lid and turn the burner on low. Carson used to eat my pasta voraciously and ask for seconds, sometimes thirds, although, to be honest, she was a much better cook. She was a much better cook because she'd eat anything. She'd eat anything because nothing scared her. But not me. I play it safe. Once when we were in the dunes she found wild mushrooms and cooked them for me. To me they were enormous chunks of rot. I refused them. She fed them to Martin who shares her uninhibited tastes.

I refill my wine glass and put Carson's postcard on the sill against the window with all the other postcards she's sent me of beaches. A few of Washington state from her time in Seattle, a bunch from California where she was living up until a week or so ago. And now these unreal photos where the heat swells off the paper. She's sleeping in her car. She's sleeping alone on the beach. She hasn't showered; she's sunburned and her lips are chapped and peeling. She's eating coconuts off the street.

Martin pushes his bowl around the kitchen with his nose. He's probably remembering the fish head he found on the beach. Or the mushrooms he ate because I wouldn't. When he finally decides there's really no more food, he settles himself at my feet and sighs.

～〲〱～

It didn't happen a third time. Because Carson left. Women leave me a lot. They say I don't know how to get close. That I'm distant and they feel like intruders in my life. They may be right. But Carson didn't say that when she left. She told me she'd miss me. "I don't know how to stop running," she'd said.

I stood on the sidewalk outside my apartment where she'd spent her last night. I had my hands in my pockets and my eyes were wet. I couldn't speak. Carson was gently cajoling Martin out of the back seat of her car where he'd decided to stay, his soft old face resting on a plastic bag stuffed with clothes. He looked out at me through the window. Wasn't there anything I could do? He seemed to ask. Rain turned to hail and pelted the car windows. I bent my head, but the sound of the ice on the glass grew loud inside me, and I remained silent.

～〲〱～

The wind has picked up, and rain pelts the kitchen window. I push the pasta around with a fork, turn down the burner, and cover the pot. The sausage is sizzling and popping. I add spaghetti sauce from a jar. Martin sits behind me, his ears perked up, the tips of them flopped over. Outside the river has turned dark. The lights of the bridge are lost in the vast sky. There is no sign of stars or a moon.

One night not long after Carson and I had first met, we watched the moon rise over Astoria. We were sitting on a log way out on the beach which forms the south end of the mouth of the Columbia. We looked back around the curve at our little town. The moon was huge and orange and full.

"It's like a sun," she said.

"A new beginning," I said.

"I'm so far from home," she said. "I could use a new beginning."

"Me too," I said.

"Maybe now I've finally gotten far enough away from that hell."

"Where we started from was hell," I confirmed.

We turned to look at one another. Carson's face was narrow and strong trimmed with short uneven hair she'd cut herself. The edges of her face took on the blue gray of everything surrounding her. How had she so quickly become part of this landscape? At the time I was shocked by how different we were, me with my quiet ordered life and my odd fears, and sloppy, brave Carson who couldn't manage to stay in one place.

But now, with Carson's beaches lined up against my window, I can only think how alike we are. Where we came from was hell. I take a long look out the window. For a moment I can just make out a thin, fading line of arcing lights trying to cross the Columbia. But soon enough the fog and rain pull in, and the darkness is complete.

Compliance

I work in Compliance now. This week anyway. Last week I worked in Acquisitions. I worked the phones, but they sent me to Compliance when I said, "Hello, Acquee, Acquiescence." I knew it was not acquiescence, but I was flustered. The guy on the other end of the line said, "Excuse me?" like he was insulted. I'm much happier in Compliance anyway. No phones. I'm a collator.

I'm sitting in a soft gray chair with wheels. On the table in front of me is a stack of white papers, each with a file tab at the top. The papers come in groups of five, the tabs in five different places from left to right. I also have a stack of stickers. The stickers fit neatly onto the tabs, A through J, which means two sets of tab sheets per folder. I'm collating folders for a merger. Mergers are dangerous things, messy and violent, and I'm not supposed to think about them. I'm not supposed to think about the red paint. The papers are white and crisp, and the rugs are gray, and the chair is gray, and the air is still and quiet.

Section A: Conversion Checklist

My cousin wants me to go to a party with her. I don't have anything to wear. It was hard enough finding these work clothes, business casual.

"What does that mean?" I ask my cousin.

"No jeans, no tennis shoes, no T-shirts. Nothing untucked."

I wanted to cry. I used to run naked through the woods.

My cousin took me to Penney's. She picked out two outfits and a wide black belt. Jimmy tried to hang himself with a belt. He was drunk and doped up. I remember thinking, better him than me. That was before the paint. But I'm trying not to think about mergers, about naked bodies, mine and Jimmy's, rubbing up against one another. My cousin always says, "Just stop thinking about it."

"I don't wear belts," I tell my cousin. The lights from the dressing room bring out red splotches in my skin.

"It looks cute," she said.

My stomach hurt. I bought the belt.

I stick a tab and put the sheet face down then pick up the stack and straighten it out, the edges of the papers knocking on the counter top. My cousin's irritated with me, I know. It's important to her that I wear the right clothes. So I'm wearing the right clothes. Isn't that enough? But it's important to her that I meet people too. "Anybody interesting at work?" she asked the other night. "No," I said. "Nobody."

Yesterday I worked with a girl who couldn't stop talking. The talking rattled around inside my head.

"When I did this for Group Health we did it different. It wasn't this boring. They let you do different tasks, not the same thing for hours. I can't believe they expect us to do this."

What was I supposed to say? I was quiet and happy, concentrating hard on making sure the stickers weren't crooked. I'd devised a system for pulling the stickers off the thin waxy paper. I'd fold back the edge of the row until the stickers were partially unstuck and easier to remove.

"I can't get these stickers off," she said. "The plastic is giving me a headache," she said. "The letters are too small. My eyes are going buggy. When I worked at Group Health they used bigger print." I didn't believe her. "I can't do this much longer. I'm a writer. This is not creative enough for me."

I could do this for days, months. I could watch my neat stacks of ten tab sheets pile up, one crossing the other, one canceling the other, this canceling that. Over and over and over.

Section B: Conversion Instructions and Highlights

When the manager of the merger folder project came in, the woman I was working with whispered, "Oh thank god. Something different."

"These need to be cut and inserted into the folders," the manager said. She put a green cutter and a stack of new copies on the table and left.

"Do you want to cut?" I said.

"No," my coworker said.

I was sorry to leave my tabs. Two days of tabs was not enough for me.

At first the cutter made me nervous. The papers were still warm and the ink smelled strong and sweet. I lined one sheet against the squares engraved on the cutter. The squares made me think of cubicles. Except for this room, Compliance is all cubicles. The cutting was exacting work, and I was happy again. I kept my fingers away from the blade. I swung the arm down. Whoosh. I used to run shirtless through the woods with a machete hacking at the blackberries along the paths.

"We should only have to lift these things once," the woman said as she unpacked a box of plastic binder folders and emptied them onto the table. There were twelve binders per box. There were fifty boxes. Whoosh across the top, whoosh, along the left side, the right, the bottom. The trail's a mess. My arms are scratched and covered with thin lines of red balls like spatter paint. "Emmy! Emmy!" I yell. "Emmy!" I hear rustling and I stop. The branches around me have blunt and broken ends from my summer trail blazing. "Emmy?" I see the wing of a bird in a bush. I am having a hard time breathing.

"When I worked—"

Swoosh swoosh swoosh swoosh.

I've been instructed not to think about these things, not Jimmy, not the dog, not the woods.

Section C: Equipment

My coworker didn't come in today. The manager said she called in sick. "Are you okay alone?" she said.

"Of course," I said, and I smiled and she backed out of the room.

So it's just me again. And I'm back to tabs, which makes me happy. I think about arriving at my cousin's party in my rain boots, the ones always caked with mud. This makes me laugh. I'm naked except for the boots, and there are a row of people who all look like my coworker and my manager and my cousin, and they all extend their hands, and I say, "Pleased to meet you, Pleased to meet you." I laugh out loud, "Ha." It's okay, there's no one here.

The boots are in my closet in the apartment my cousin helped me find, and I do wear them here in the city. I slip them over my bare feet in the mornings when I walk Emmy. Black rubber boots with dark red soles. Jimmy's sole was red. I saw the red bottom of his boot, and I saw the back of his flannel shirt, and I saw the door bounce twice against the frame after he slammed it. On the wood floor is a circle of red paint, a circle that leaks out little drips in many directions. Dust and dog hair are stuck to the paint. A red boot print, then half a red boot print, then the outline of the right side of a boot lead to the door. Outside the door, new green blackberry shoots lie across the crooked boards of the porch. In a small bit of sky, a cloud is rapidly moving.

The door of the room I work in is open, but still, there is little air here. Nothing moves but my hands, yellow in the steady light. I'm in the back room at what is usually a conference table. There are large windows that look out at other windows of other eighth-floor rooms.

Section D: Cash and Negotiables

"I'm selling my TV over the web," a woman says. Though the door is open, I can't see her cubicle.

"Any luck?" another woman says.

"Three messages, I'm just checking them now."

"What are you asking?"

"$50. The remote doesn't work. But I need enough to buy this one that's on sale at Freddy's."

Where is this web anyway? A word assigned to nothing. The woods. A word assigned to a cluster of trees, alder and hemlock and fir, and dirt and beetles and worms and robins and squirrels and slugs. The superhighway. Words in an unknown space. My driveway. The end of an old logging road. Baby alders crowd the edges. Small bugs balance on the surface of muddy puddles out of which truck tire tracks emerge. I'm in the kitchen cooking cabbage and rice. Jimmy's truck pulls up as I throw another log in the barrel-shaped woodstove. Emmy is curled up between the kindling box and the stove, the brown tip of her tail tucked under her wiry, white chin.

"What have you got to lose? You should get what you can for it." A file cabinet opens.

"That's how I see it."

Section E: Wire Transfer Instructions

The manager comes in. "There's a call for you," she says. I pick up the phone in the conference room.

"You're coming tonight, right?" my cousin says.

"Yeah," I say.

"Do you want me to pick you up at work?"

"I have to walk Emmy," I say.

"Jesus, Lucille, not that again."

I stare out at floor number eight of the building across a span of air. Cubicles? Probably. "I have to get dressed," I add.

"Okay, fine," she says. "Any great guys where you work?"

"No," I say. "None. I have to get back to work."

"Seven?"

"Good."

In the conference room, boxes are stacked neatly against the walls and under the table. Tab sheets are stacked neatly on the table. The room smells of new plastic. The cutter with its violent green arm is on the window sill beside the stapler and hole puncher. The drawers are filled with hundreds of ordered files. In my apartment clothes are tumbling out of my drawers, dirty clothes are heaped on the floor, and shirts are hanging on the chairs.

When we lived in the cabin Jimmy used to leave his plaid and chamois shirts on the chair by the blue table in the area that was our kitchen. I'd play with the buttons, slide the round plastic between the cloth slit, in and out, as if there were somebody inside.

I touch my thumb to the sticky upturned edge of a label then place the label as straight as possible on a tab.

Section F: Frequently Used Procedures

I hold one page of eight-tab sticker sets in my right hand. With my left, because I am left handed, I pull the tabs off of their waxy backing. The pile of tab sets waiting to be stuck is on my right. I drop the empty wax paper, with just the edges of sticker remaining, into a waste basket to the right of my seat.

Directly in front of me is the pile of blank file divider sheets, the tabs parallel to the edge of the table. After I stick each sticker, I slide the sheet above the pile, and after ten sheets, one completed set, I straighten the stack and add it to the criss-crossed stack to my left. I put that pile beyond the reach of my elbow because when I first started, I knocked the pile onto the floor.

I devised this system within my first hour in Compliance, and I find it is the most efficient method. I found I worked twice as fast as my coworker who had papers in disarray around her and misplaced tab stickers all over her fingers. I worried that she would destroy the order I had created.

Jimmy's standing beside the woodstove yelling. I have lost track of the words. The paint on the kitchen table is chipped and peeling. There are dust balls in the corners. A leg of the propane burner is uneven and I worry about fires. Blackberries grow through the railroad ties which are the cabin walls, and I can see small pinpoints of light shining through. Jimmy kicks the dog with the inside of his boot. The dog leaves the ground, all four of her paws leave the ground, and her head when she comes down hits the dusty wood floor.

There is nothing dusty here. The machines run smoothly, and they hum. I hear the copier sometimes, far away, behind a door and a partition. The muffled sound of fingers on keyboards is so regular it sounds like a slow motor.

Section G: Resources

I work until 4:30, but I wouldn't mind working until 9. At nine I could take the bus and be back at my apartment before 10. At

10 I could at least lie down. I could pretend to sleep. At 5:30, you can't pretend to sleep. If I were here until 9, I wouldn't have to maneuver through the people on the streets. I wouldn't have to apologize and step out of the way. At 9 there are not many cars, and in the dark it is harder to tell how everything is broken up into tiny squares; the sidewalks, the buildings, even people's faces become part of a complex system.

But tonight I am going to a party. I wonder if I will meet people like my coworker and my manager and the woman selling her TV on the superhighway. I stood on the porch, my hand shading my eyes, "Emmy!" I called. I stare at the screen of a TV buried in blackberry vines. In it Emmy is suspended in air; her yelp is suspended; her eyes frantic and rolling in their sockets.

The phone rings. I press a tab onto paper. The windows of the building across the street are mirrored. The phone rings again. A mouse scampers past the woodstove. Rain drums the cabin, and wind blows through the cracks in the walls. My hands are covered with red paint. I am wrapped in a blue comforter that is also splattered with tear-shaped spots of red. The woodstove is cold. The cabin smells of rot. I think I have been sitting like this for days but I'm not sure. The phone rings again.

After all, my cousin did find me the apartment. She did pay the rent Jimmy and I were behind on at the cabin, though it wasn't half the amount I pay here. Jimmy sure wouldn't have paid it. He took off. Never even called. He doesn't know where I am now, and that's okay—the counselor says, that's okay. My cousin really has been helpful, which is more than I can say for some people—she did put down my first and last, and she did provide herself as my reference. The phone continues to ring, and I continue to stick tabs. I suppose I could pretend to enjoy myself this evening.

Section H: Customer Communications

My manager stands in the doorway. "What's the problem?" she says.

I look up. "What?"

"I just called here."

"I didn't know I was supposed to answer the phone," I say.

She's wearing a red suit jacket. I did not buy a red suit jacket. I bought a blue sweater with a v-neck and a white button-up shirt I had to tuck in.

"I have something else for you to do," she says.

I panic, but she doesn't notice.

"Is this part of the merger?" I ask.

"It's not a merger," she says. "It's a conversion. We don't call them mergers. How many times do I have to tell you?"

I don't say anything. I'm thinking how when Jimmy's body merged with mine, perhaps that too was a conversion? I'm thinking, what happened to the word merger? I see it out there on the superhighway, maneuvering around all the other lost words.

"These coversheets need to be slipped under the binder covers. The binders are in those boxes."

"I know," I say. "The other woman counted them."

"Right." She puts a stack of bright orange cardstock on the table. The cardstock announces the conversion in bold letters.

Section I: Reference Materials

I decide not to do the binders today. Perhaps I can do them tomorrow. She did not say they needed to be done today. I still have many tabs to stick, at least three hours' worth, and there are only two hours left today. The bright orange in the middle of the table is disturbing, so I put the stack of cardstock in one of the boxes with the binders.

From the top of the steps going up to the loft I could see the splot of red paint below. It is drying a dark brown. Unfolded clothes are piled on metal shelving. The plastic protecting the broken window flaps and rattles. "Emmy?" I say as I approach the bed. She is lying on her side, one white and brown paw jutting out over the edge of the bed. I crouch beside her and pet her coarse fur. "Emmy?" I pick up one of Jimmy's shirts from the floor and gather her in my arms. I wrap the shirt around her body. I button it. The sheets and the comforter are covered with red paint. There are spots on the pillow. In my arms Emmy is heavy, stiff, and still.

I cannot stick tabs anymore. I cannot stand the tackiness on my fingers. I cannot stand that there is no air. I breathe deep but the breath stops halfway to my lungs. I put my palms flat on the table. My hands, yellow in the florescence, twitch and jump.

Section J: Products and Services

I am able to negotiate with myself. I am able to swallow the breath. I stare at the tab stickers. The black letters leap off the pages and switch places with each other so that I cannot read them. How easily they could get up and walk out.

"What does that mean?" I asked my cousin. "Talent Tree. Is this is a real thing?"

"Hang up, Lucille. Enough already. You'll like it just fine. They're a good agency."

I imagine people hanging on trees, and people in red jackets pick them and package them in business casual shirts and sell them. There is a place in the city where I hang on a tree. I am out on the thinnest branch in the coldest part of winter, but I do not feel the cold.

Emmy used to come with me through the woods when I did trail maintenance. Light filtered in through the trees, and leaf patterns moved across the ground. I'd often peel off my shirt because there was no one around for miles, and the damp air felt good against my skin. The leaves brushed by my bare shoulders. Emmy chased birds in the brush; she growled and shook at roots believing them to be sticks she could dislodge from the earth. She'd run ahead on the trail then stop and look back, waiting for me. Maybe she's the only one who ever really waited for me. I look out the window and imagine her square little terrier face peering at me through tall grass. For the first time I notice clouds above the sky-scrapers. They are gathering and parting, gathering and parting.

My Old Man

My boy Quentin and I take walks in the morning. He shuffles and stops often to cough and lean on the wood cane Dr. Brad gave him before we left the city. The steady sound of the creek is always all around us, and the air smells of dry grass. Quentin is happier here than in the city, and so am I. I told my supervisor at CARE Center I didn't want to work full-time anymore, and I didn't want to work mornings.

It's surprising how you can tell someone what you want and you actually get it. I worked ten years in the city without asking for anything. Now I'm asking all the time. Quentin's taught me a lot about that. I mean, I wouldn't have asked if it weren't for him, not for myself I wouldn't have asked. They gave me a break on my benefits too, said they'd consider it kind of a sick leave. I know my supervisor's bending the rules, but I'm getting better at taking gifts from people. Besides, she's seen Quentin leaning on his red cane with the wolf-head handle. She said to my Quentin, "What an angel you are."

I wonder how far he will walk today as I pause to wait for him. We've just passed our living room windows, big squares that face the dusty road. One curtain is partially open and inside I see our table, two wooden folding chairs, and Quentin's small red bed in the corner by the window. Besides the bathroom and kitchen, we just have two rooms in this house, his room and mine. There's an upstairs I thought I could clean up so Quentin could have his own room, but since the second bout of pneumonia, he gets too winded climbing the steps. So he gets the living room, which is good because it has nice light, not too bright but kind of yellow in the mornings. You can see the shadow of the maple tree on the carpet. Quentin likes that. "Look, Momma," he says some mornings. "The leaves are here in my room."

"Imagine that," I say.

Quentin stops and outlines the shadows of leaves in the gravel with his cane. The maple leaves above our heads have just begun to turn yellow. Behind them the blue sky just doesn't stop.

"Messasatize," Quentin says and walks on.

"Metastasize," I say. We've been working on this all morning.

"Messass—" he coughs and gags, stops, and with his free hand, hits his chest briskly three times then coughs again.

"You don't need to say it."

"But what if it's happening? Shouldn't I know how to say it? It's in me, right?" He says these things all day long. The dusty air makes my eyes sting. Quentin's supposed to be the one with the bad stomach, but I don't ever want to eat after hearing him choking on a word like that. What's a seven-year-old gotta know about big words like that anyway?

"You'll be fine, Quentin," I say.

We walk past our neighbor's mailbox which is nailed to a tree, and Quentin says, "When does the mail come to our house, Momma?"

"Noon, Honey," I say, "usually around noon."

"I always miss it."

I can't imagine what he's waiting for.

"You nap then, Quentin," I say. "Can you see any glass today?"

He's standing in our neighbor's driveway. At the end of the drive is a barn converted into a work place. "There's something red hanging from a tree. It looks like a flame," he says. "It's the shape of a flame."

"Or a huge drop of water," I say. Our neighbor is a glass blower.

"But it's red," he says.

"A berry," I suggest.

"It's a flame."

A few houses from our house, past the glass blower's house and the house with the boat and the fishing buoys on all the trees, is a small bridge over our creek. When we cross the bridge, Quentin stops to lean over. Below us the creek forms a deep pool. At the beginning of the summer, when we first moved here, for recovery we'd thought, we'd hoped, but that was before the pneumonia, and I was working fulltime, keeping up with bills, no borrowed money; at the beginning of the summer we climbed down the rocks and Quentin went swimming in that pool. It's hard to imagine now, him scrambling over rocks, me holding his hand, his bare chest dipping into the clearness.

"Grasshopper to butterfly," he says real fast as a grasshopper flies up in front of us, kicking up the slightest bit of powdery dust. It's a game we play, who can say it first. The grasshoppers were the first thing Quentin noticed when we moved here. He used to stalk around hitting the dust with his cane and poking it into the meadow grass.

He crosses to the other side of the bridge and rests his chin on the cement rail. The pair of herons we've been watching appears from out of a scraggy pine on the opposite bank. They coast low over the water. Up on the canyon rim a train moves slowly. Quentin says, "You can still hear the creek underneath the train."

"Yep, you're right." I watch him watching the water. I watch him listening for the steady sound of the water that not even the train can drown out. I think about the steady beat of his heart and how all the blood in his body just keeps flowing, and what a strong little guy he is inside, and I think maybe, just maybe, he'll stay alive. The creek is lit up with spots of white light. I can hear it too, filling the whole space in my head as if there were nothing else in there, filling my hungry stomach, washing away the nausea, loosening the tightness.

"I'm hungry," Quentin says. "Could we go home and make grilled cheese sandwiches?"

I want to question him. Can you really eat that? But I don't. I believe him. He can. I want him to. I just have to ask for what I want, right?

—⟋⟍—

Quentin can't eat the grilled cheese sandwich. He sits at the wooden table with his favorite blue plate in front of him. The windows and doors are open so we can hear the creek. He looks down at the sandwich. The cheese has dripped onto the plate and turned a dark yellow. He doesn't even pick it up and try to bite around the edge or poke at it with his finger. He just looks at it and starts to cry. And when he cries, he chokes and he coughs.

"Okay, Quentin," I say looking at the sandwich that makes me ill now too. "Why don't you nap a bit? We can try some applesauce later." I touch his slouched back; I put both my hands on his shoulders. They feel like the shoulders of a little skeleton. "Quentin, Honey," I say. I put both my arms around him, rest my chin across his head, and hug him, careful not to hug too tight. He coughs and gags. "Some rest, okay?" I help him out of his chair, put my arm around him, and guide him to his bed.

He crawls under the covers. "I'm hungry," he says. His face tightens up. "My stomach hurts," he says. He curls into a ball and pulls the blanket over his face.

I stroke the lump of his shoulder and back, "Shssss. Quiet Quentin. Relax. I know it hurts. Relax." Though he holds on tight, he's still a seven-year-old, and he does fall asleep quickly. Life tires him out. He falls asleep now, and his legs stretch out, and his sleeping face appears from beneath the covers. His hair has thinned. The hospital kept him in the children's ward through most of the chemo. It was a dismal place full of shadowy children and weeping parents. A woman came around with puppets, but most of the kids were too sick to care. Our apartment was empty without him, so I just stopped going home. I'd go from work to the hospital and back to work. I worried that he'd never leave there. But with Quentin, the chemo had stuck, and eventually we came home. Some people are lucky. We thought Quentin was lucky. That's when Dr. Pope, Quentin's Dr. Brad, and I talked about moving him. He said Quentin would be happier if I were happier. He said his recovery could depend on his happiness. It was the only thing we could control, so why not control it? He said words like fresh air and quiet and walks in the country and less stress. I didn't think doctors said those things anymore. My sister lives near here, and maybe we don't get along, but she likes Quentin, and besides, I've learned to ask for the things I want— like job transfers, loans, time off.

I always thought you should be happy with what you've got and that's it. That's all you get. But now I'm beginning to understand sometimes you aren't always dealt what you need. Everything was want to me, and want was selfish. God gave you what you have. It should be enough. Quentin doesn't believe in God. He's seven, and he doesn't believe in God. I suppose it's my fault. Maybe I didn't stop believing in Him, but I sure stopped caring about Him.

Quentin rolls on his side. They say pneumonia is a friend of the very old and the very ill. Though Quentin is very ill, I mostly see how very old he is. I see a wise old man in his closed eyes. I see his life ahead as if it were here, as if the whole timeline were in one place, the boy Quentin, the man Quentin, what he could be, what he isn't yet, what he might not be. You might say it's his soul I'm seeing, the rest of him. His arm is crossed over the front of him. He's partway between lying on his side and partway lying on his stomach. His shoulder juts up larger than usual, like a man's, like the sleeping shoulders of lovers I've had. I want to draw his shoulder, the angle of it as it slopes toward the turning arm on one side and the plane of the back on the other.

No lover I ever had was wise. I guess I always figured, this is just what you get. Most people learn how to tell a good lover from a bad one sometime in their twenties. They learn lovers should give to you as much as you give to them, that love is not about pouring in until all your pouring is gone. Not me though, I never figured that out, at least not in practice. I was 32 when I met Quentin's father; he was 46. I'd been alone a long time. I moved in with Richard within a month of meeting him, got pregnant the next month, woke up one day, and he was gone. The TV was gone. The stereo. My car, gone. I gagged on my toothbrush that morning and threw up in the sink. For a week I had the same dream: I was standing on a hospital table swinging a machete at an enormous snake. I cut the snake's head off, and, horrified, dropped to the ground to try to revive it. It turned into Quentin's father. He was laughing at me. "Stupid," he said, putting my face between his palms and squeezing until I could hear my skull cracking.

All I can hear now is Quentin's quiet, raspy breath and the sound of the creek stumbling over rocks and moving on. I go to the kitchen and fill a glass with Talking Rain, lime-flavored carbonated water, Quentin's favorite I-have-a-stomachache drink. I put it on the carpet beside his bed. Then I pull Pentels and a drawing pad out from under his bed. He likes Pentels better than crayons because they smear. I pull out the black and the white and get a wad of toilet paper from the bathroom. I begin to draw the outline of my son's body, erasing the stray black lines with the white, muting the sharp lines with the toilet paper, until eventually just a hint of his spirit begins to appear in the white spaces.

I push the pad and Pentels back under the bed, pour myself a glass of Quentin's Talking Rain, and go outside to work in the garden. In another hour, Quentin and I will have to go back to the doctor. The doctor is someone Dr. Pope recommended. X-rays were taken during his hospitalization for pneumonia, and now we have to go back for ultrasound and more blood tests. He may need a biopsy or another CAT scan. We won't know until the doctor tells us what he sees. We know what the emergency room doctor thinks he sees.

Quentin's cane is leaning against the wall in the corner by the door. The red wolfhead looks at me. I turn and look back at Quentin. I don't want to wake him in an hour. He will be in pain and crying. He will be even more hungry and even more sick to his stomach. He will not want to sit in the hot car. He will complain when he hears the traffic. But we need to find out what's going on inside of him so we can get rid of it.

I pull a garlic from the fridge and carry it out into the yard. Each day at Quentin's nap time, I dig up plant beds that are years overgrown with grass and weeds. There are two circular beds in front of the house, each surrounded by a cement ring. Yesterday I finished digging up the first bed. Today I get to plant. I picture spring with Quentin and me on the porch and the fat round purple garlic flowers rattling in a light breeze. The lawn is bright green, and the creek is twice as fat and twice as high and twice as loud as it is now. Quentin is eating a Ho Ho and giggling. Chocolate is smeared on his face. He is a normal boy.

Today the lawn is brittle and brown, and meadow grass grows along the fence line. I've cut the tops off the irises that were in bloom when we arrived. I kneel down in the round space of dirt with a trowel, tear the garlic into cloves, and bury them. I want my boy to live.

—⁓—

Quentin is sitting on a hospital bed wrapped in a white sheet. His feet off the edge of the bed are crossed and his legs are bent at the knees. He hugs the sheet close to his body. "Quentin, why don't you get dressed while I go to the bathroom?" I say. This past year he has preferred to dress himself in private.

He nods but doesn't speak.

"Have a cotton ball," I say picking up a glass jar of cotton balls and holding it out to him.

He doesn't laugh even though he's usually the one offering me the cotton ball, or the tongue depressor, or the rubber glove.

"Not feeling so well, are you?"

He shakes his head.

"Okay, Sweetie," I say and touch his face. "I'll be quick."

The nurse has gone to get the doctor, and there's no telling when she'll get back. I stop off in the lobby and pick up *Caleb and Kate*, Quentin's favorite book from this particular waiting room. On my way back to the examining room, I find him sitting on a bench in the hallway just past the waiting room.

"What are you doing here?" I say. I sit down beside him and put my arm around his thin shoulders.

"The nurse said," he mumbles with his face down.

"That you're finished?"

He nods. The nurse, however, is walking briskly toward us. "There you are," she says. "I worried when I saw the examining room empty."

"We're not done?" I say.

"Well, no." The nurse is confused, but I am not.

"Quentin," I say. "We need to go back in. We're not done yet."

The nurse holds out her hand to him. "I have some sourballs in the examining room," she says.

But Quentin slips onto the floor and crawls under the bench. I look down at *Caleb and Kate*, the cover a watercolor of an old woman and a dog, then up at the nurse whose neck has broken out in red splotches.

"Quentin," I say. But he doesn't answer. He's crying. I slip onto the floor, and on hands and knees, peer under the black bench. He's pressed against the wall. There is fear and stubborn refusal in his red face. His eyes are wide and he's pinching his arms. My eyes well up. I look over my shoulder at the nurse and say, "I want to talk to the doctor, now."

"I'll get him," she says. "I'm sorry," she says. But I've turned away and am sitting on the floor waiting for Quentin to come out.

Finally, he grips my arm and crawls into my lap. "I'm hungry," he says and vomits. His face is against my shoulder and his arms around my neck. His skin is hot and damp and his arms boney.

A woman wheels around us in a wheelchair. She looks down at us briefly and then quickly rolls on. The doctor and the nurse find Quentin and me still sitting on the floor. The red splotches immediately reappear on the nurse's neck when she sees the vomit. She hurries off for towels.

"He's running a fever," I say. "Will he be alright? Is it the pneumonia again?" There is a tightness in my throat, and I wonder if I've been crying this whole time, or is it just now that I've started? I feel dizzy and extremely tired.

"He'll be fine for now," the doctor says. "His lungs are actually clearing up. He's probably just upset. Get fluids in him, and let him sleep. Keep him on the antibiotics."

"Okay," I say, but I don't know if I actually say it. I know I nod my head. The white hallway walls curve inward. My nose is running, but my hands have vomit on them. I wish for a moment I didn't have to get up off that floor, that someone would come and check both Quentin and me into a white room, put IVs in our arms, and let us drift away and not come back. I try to think of the creek.

"We have to go home," I say.

When I stand up with the weight of Quentin in my arms, the curve of my spine aches. He is hugging my neck and burying his face into my chest.

"I understand," the doctor says. "I'll take a look at the blood work when it comes back. Why don't you call me Thursday afternoon? It's likely we'll still need a CAT scan."

Quentin hates the CAT scan. After the first scan he woke up screaming every night for a week. In the day he'd tell me how the tunnel was really a snake pit, and he had to go through it. Something would move in the grass, or the hedge would shake with a breeze, and Quentin would run inside and hide under his bed. For days I couldn't get him as far as the sidewalk outside our city apartment.

It occurs to me that we can't go through that again. It occurs to me that I might not want to know the results of another CAT scan. I might not want to live with the shadowy little boy the surgery and chemo will leave behind. I do not want to revisit the fear of the children's ward—that he will never leave it. We've already been through all this.

The nurse returns with a damp towel and Quentin's cane. "Thank you," I say. I put the towel over my shoulder and carry the cane.

"He's a real sweetheart," the nurse says. "We'll see you later."

I wonder.

We leave without stopping at the front desk.

"Momma," Quentin says, as we walk out the glass doors.

"Yes, Honey?"

But he coughs, and his cough is phlegmy, and then he gags and dry heaves. When we get to the car, I lean the cane against the hood, dig the keys out of my pocket, and open the passenger side. I sit Quentin up on the seat, holding his shoulder with one hand and wiping his face with the damp cloth with the other. I hand him his cane and swing his legs into the seat then shut the door. Gray surrounds his eyes. His narrow chin (it didn't used to be that thin) quivers.

On the drive home he sleeps with his head in my lap clutching his cane. The wolf face is pressed against his chest. I know it's unsafe, but I don't care. The car is hot and everything smells of vomit. I bawl the entire drive home.

—\\\—

I sit on the porch and watch tiny bugs flutter in the dusty yellow light. There are thousands of them. I sit for hours watching them while Quentin sleeps inside. I am like a rock in the creek. The water moves around me, and I remain perfectly still.

I turn my head slowly, and Quentin is standing beside me. He has a crooked, sleepy smile on his face, and his eyes are still partially closed and puffy. He's wearing heavy wool socks, blue pajama bottoms, and a white T-shirt. He's holding the glass of Talking Rain I put beside his bed earlier in the day, but he has obviously refilled it.

"Want a sip?" he says.

"Thanks," I say. The phizzy water works its way into my numb and quiet stomach. I put the glass down and put my palm on the side of his face. He doesn't feel feverish anymore. "How are you feeling?"

"Fine," he says. "I had nice dreams."

"Really?"

"Yes. I was a grasshopper that turned into a butterfly. I flew above our creek."

"That's lovely, Quentin."

"Want a cracker?" He holds out a handful of saltines.

"Have you been eating those?"

"Uh huh."

"Good boy."

"Want one?"

"I think I do." I take a saltine from his outstretched palm. It melts into a bland, salty bread in my mouth.

"Can we go down to the creek?"

"Are you sure you're up to it?" I'm thinking that just in the last week he spent two days without once getting out of bed and two days where he never made it past the porch. Does he really mean this? He hasn't had this much activity in one day for over a month.

"It's not very far," he says.

"Okay, Kiddo. Put on your tennis shoes and a sweatshirt."

While Quentin is inside, I look about our yard, the new circle of fresh dirt, the small chicken-wire fence, the dilapidated chicken coops and the patch of silvery creek. I look at the porch and the rocking chair, the maple tree. I live in a house. I am 39 years old, and for the first time since I was a child, I live in a house. A house with a yard and a creek. I have a place where a boy can chase grasshoppers. Having is not taking.

"I'm ready," Quentin says.

"Where's your cane?"

"Don't need it. You'll hold my hand on the rocky part?"

"Of course I will."

We cross the yard, pass the chicken coops, and head down the trail to the creek. Quentin picks a large yellow leaf off the ground and holds it up to me.

"The first one," he says. "It's a letter to me."

"Yeah? What does it say?"

"It says, 'Dear Quentin.'"

"Is that all?"

"Uh huh." Quentin carries the leaf with him.

The trail leads through dry meadow grass and an occasional sage bush. Quentin stops and rubs the sage into his fingers then smells his fingers as we go along. The trail passes through sandy patches by the creek and then is rocky where the creek rises in winter. We've cleared a path through the tall river grass and winter river bed which leads right to the edge of the creek. In the summer, we'd wade into the creek and sit on rocks in the center of it, but now we sit on our regular rocks on the edge. Quentin plays with the water with his fingers.

"Quentin," I say. "Dr. Marshall thinks you should have another CAT scan."

He doesn't say anything. He doesn't even look at me. He watches the wakes his fingers make in the water.

"Quentin," I say, "do you remember what happened today at the hospital?"

"No," he says absently. "Look, Momma, a little snake!" He points at one of the rocks we usually sit on in the creek. A tiny snake head is poised out of the water, still and frightened. "It's a baby," Quentin whispers when he realizes how frightened it is of us. Slowly, the snake lowers its head back into the water. We watch the small body just below the surface ride downstream with the current.

"Wow," Quentin whispers. "I don't want a CAT scan," he says. "I don't want that. I don't want to go back to the hospital."

An evening breeze rises off the creek, touches my hand, and moves up my arm. Along the banks upstream red and yellow leaves shiver. I want to object, but I trust Quentin. "Alright," I say. "No more hospitals."

The creek stumbles along into winter. I try to remember a time when his cheeks were filled out, when he had one low dimple beneath the left corner of his mouth. Now his face is so small that his eyes appear larger. For a moment, I see him as others see him, not as I see him everyday—and I am alarmed by the strangeness of him: he is gaunt and shriveled like a shrunken old man, the skin around his eyes ashen. Even his hands are tiny. His enormous eyes seem to drift away and drift back, away and back, as if he has already begun looking beyond the creek and our little house, beyond the grasshoppers, beyond October's swarms of dust-sized bugs. It is as if I have been given the gift of distance, if only briefly. And then, just as suddenly, he is Quentin again, cocking his head like a curious little boy, the ghost of a dimple dying to show itself. He is looking back at me, fully present. There is a secret in his dark eyes, and the secret is just between him and me. It is thin as the veins on a red leaf, elusive as the dust that disappears after the leaf finally crumbles. In that look, I know that he understands exactly what he's said, and never in my life would I stand in the way of what my boy wants.

My Doppelganger's Arms

When I first saw her, she was wearing a long-sleeved, white T-shirt and gray men's cotton pants rolled up almost to her knees. She was carrying a white Styrofoam cup with a lid and a straw as she walked along the beach. I noticed her from far off because she looked so aimless, not like someone walking briskly down the beach, straight any way you look at it. She waded into the water as the tide pulled in over the bottoms of her pants. I thought how odd to roll one's pants up and still not move away when the water washes over them.

I watched the woman from inside a driftwood hut built up against the dune. She was down the beach and to my left. The knots in the driftwood looked like eyes. The pieces, crossing one another, formed shapes that appeared to be more than one thing at the same time. I saw a bird that could also be a woman, and two birds that were one. There was a small fire ring, a table made of a thick stump and a board flaked with red paint, and an empty wine bottle. There was just room enough for one person only to curl up and sleep.

The woman was wading out into the water again. When I was a child and my parents and I were staying in a hotel overlooking the ocean, I saw a woman walk into the water. It was dark, and I was unsure of what I was watching. Still, it seemed as if she waded straight out and didn't come back. I watched for a long time. My parents were out as usual. I never told them.

I squatted in the driftwood hut until the sun went down and the sky behind me turned pink. Then I headed over the dunes' trail and to my truck. She was sitting on the curb lifting her foot up, staring at it. The cup had blown over, and something had spilled onto the parking lot. There were no other cars, no bike. The beach was at least five miles from any house. The woman started slapping her foot. She appeared to be about my age. Although I watched her from not too far off, she didn't look up once. Until I went over to her.

I went over because, like I said, she looked about my age. In fact, she looked like someone who might be my close friend. Only perhaps she was in some trouble—someone had stolen her bike or she'd missed her ride.

"Excuse me," I said, standing over her. "Are you all right? I mean, do you need a ride or anything?"

She looked up. "I stepped on something." The liquid on the parking lot was red wine. "Like a cigarette?"

She had a round face and a straightforward expression, very unlike the ambling person I'd watched on the shore. It was her frankness and her deep voice that made me say, "Sure," and sit down on the curb beside her.

"Drum okay?" she said.

"Yeah, I like Drum a lot." Which is true. I like rolling it, how wet it is, how compact.

She stood up and reached in her back pocket. Her pants were wet halfway up her thighs, and her legs were unshaven. Mine too. She handed me the crumpled Drum packet and sat back down. I rolled the paper quickly between my fingers, tight and thick. She pulled matches out of her breast pocket and lit my cigarette for me.

"Thanks," I said.

"You live around here?"

"In Astoria," I said.

"Me too."

"Yeah?"

"Uh huh, in Uniontown."

"Me too," I said.

"I'm Mar, by the way."

"M-A-R? Is that short for anything?"

"Short for Mary. My mom came up with it. She used to say Mar instead of Mare. Mar, like the sea, she'd say."

"That's nice. I'm Robin."

"You lived here long?"

"About a year. I moved from Kansas."

"Why'd you come here? Highest suicide rate in the country, you know."

I didn't know how to answer the question. "I like the ocean. There's no ocean in Topeka." My response felt like a lie. "I guess I just needed to get out of there."

"Hmmmm." She put the Styrofoam cup upright.

I watched the red wine run down the side of the cup.

"You ever go to the Portway?" Mar asked.

"I've been there a few times. I like walking down the path before dark and sitting in there with a book. But I haven't lived here long so I really don't know too many other places. It feels okay there."

"You want to go now?"

"Yeah, all right. That'd be fun. How's your foot?"

"Oh, it's fine." She stubbed her cigarette out on the curb, and so did I. I unlocked the truck and let her in.

As we drove out of the parking lot I asked her how she'd gotten to the beach.

"I'm not sure," she said. "I come out here a lot."

"Yeah, me too. It's the first place I came when I moved here, before I even found an apartment." As we drove through the dunes, Mar rested her forehead against the window as if she were tired. I thought to ask why she didn't have shoes, if she wanted a sweater. It was getting cold, and her pants were wet. But I didn't ask these things. I was happy to have her in the truck with me. She had a face that I can see inside me even when it's turned away.

I didn't have any friends in Astoria. I was living in a small town which was new to me and I was a little scared to get close to people, scared to let them know things about me. But with Mar I felt good right away, and I wanted to do what I could to keep her around. Sometimes with people you just know.

I parked in the back of the Portway. Before we got out Mar said, "I feel really dumb about this, but do you have a pair of shoes I could borrow?"

"Sure, I keep all sorts of extra stuff behind the seat. I've got a sweater too, if you want that."

"That'd be great," she said. "I feel pretty stupid for being so out of it."

"It's all right," I said.

I looked out through round boat windows at fog skidding under the light of streetlamps. Mar bought us a pitcher of Red Hook with a ten-dollar bill she'd pulled out of her back pocket. On her for the ride and the shoes, she said. "Oh, and for the sweater." We both laughed. The only sweater I had in the truck was rust-colored with five buttons and a wide flapping '70s collar. I'd gotten it at a thrift store because I thought it was funky. But I'd never actually worn it. Mar thought it was a hoot, and I told her she could have it.

"The sweater was only a quarter," I said looking up from my beer. In the pale light of the bar, Mar's face was dark with sun and soft around the edges. Stray bits of hair fell across her forehead. She looked like a child who'd gotten lost at the beach.

"Smells like it," Mar said, and we both laughed some more.

At first we were the only people in the bar, and the bartender kept glancing at Mar. His expression was at once curious and surprised. I got the feeling he thought she was cute, and it made me happy to be with her.

"Where do you work?" I said.

"The frame shop downtown."

"Oh, I got a print there. They have some great stuff."

"What'd you get?"

"You know that Picasso of the girl with the bird cupped in her palms?"

"I love that print. I mean, I'm not wild about all of his stuff, but some of it just knocks me out. That print always reminds me of the Dali of the young woman standing on the hillside, her back facing out and her hand on her hip—you know the one? I don't know what it is, but I always think of those two paintings together."

"I know the painting you mean." I felt myself getting excited, the beer bubbling up into my head. "I never thought of that before, but they do make quite a pair."

"I ordered that Dali print a while back, but it never came. I was pretty disappointed. I wanted to do a display with the two prints." Mar looked away, kind of dazed, and maybe frightened. Then she said, "But perhaps I won't have my job come Monday."

"Why not?"

"I didn't show up today, and I didn't call or anything."

"Oh."

"I've been a little forgetful recently. Well, I guess you could call it worse than that." She was still looking away from me.

Two men came in the bar and passed by our table. Both of them looked at Mar. Their pants were wet and had long dark streaks down the legs as if they'd wiped their hands on their knees over and over again. They smelled like fish oil and diesel. Perhaps they noticed that Mar's pants were also wet and dirty.

I watched the two men leaning over the bar toward the bartender. I heard the bartender say, "I know."

"Do you draw?" I said.

"Oh, yeah, I do. I was an art major in college. Have you seen that poster around town for that art contest the Arts Association put on? The shapes coming in on the surf?"

I stared at Mar unbelieving. I'd noticed that poster everywhere. Three shapes in primary colors, a circle, a square, and a triangle were washing in on the surf, and in the distance were identical shapes, only smaller, also washing in on the surf. The painting implied that behind the second set of shapes, there could be a third and a fourth, as many sets of shapes, in fact, as there are sets of waves. Every time I saw it I felt disturbed. At first I couldn't figure out why, until I decided it was because it felt so impossible and yet so clearly present, a bold statement about what was not. It made you shrink inside to see the world that way. "Sure, I've seen that."

"That's mine." She took a sip of beer.

The pitcher was almost gone, and the bartender was looking our way.

"Let's go," Mar said.

"Okay."

"Goodnight," she called to the bartender, and we left.

I left my truck in the parking lot because my place was close, and both of us liked walking up the paths in the hillside. We walked down to the Uniontown Peddler, got a six-pack, and headed up the dark trail to my apartment. Blackberries grabbed at the cuffs of my pants. It was funny how we didn't even talk about her coming over. She just came, and I expected that.

My apartment was warm and bright. Mar remarked immediately on my print of Hopper's *Rooms by the Sea*. There's an empty room with just shadows and a doorway that opens to only water. The rooms are clearly the rooms of a house—solid, rooms that wouldn't rock; however, the view from the door makes you feel as if you're looking out from inside a boat. "Sometimes my place feels like this," she said, gesturing toward the print. "Sometimes I feel like this," she added in her gravelly voice.

"Listen," Mar said as I came out of the kitchen with two open beers. "I really appreciate you taking me into town tonight. I wasn't real sure how I was going to get back."

"Well, you seemed a little, oh, confused or something."

"I've been real confused. Things happen, and then I don't remember them, except there's always, oh, you know, a mark or something to let me know they happened. And my stomach's been pretty messed up. Sometimes I can eat, and other times I can't." I looked straight into her face to see if I could recognize anything bizarre, unusual, crooked. She looked concerned, even a little frightened, but mostly just earnest. I didn't say anything.

"Well, anyway, thanks. This is a really fun evening, too. I'm having a lot of fun."

"Me too," I said, happy to leave behind whatever it was she was trying to tell me.

That night I told Mar everything about the books I'd recently read, the hikes I'd taken since I'd moved here, my visits to the mooring basin where I'd watch the seals piled on top of one another. I told her about my drive from Topeka to Astoria, how in the desert I'd seen thousands of blackbirds, like shadows of each other, repeating themselves in a widening funnel across the sky. I told her how I couldn't see the end.

I asked her if she'd been down the coast, had she seen the dunes? The seal caves? I heard myself chatting endlessly, desperate to talk. Which I was. I told her too many women my age around here were married, settled, pregnant, and I felt out of place. I came here to rest and walk on the beach. I was happy to be out here, but I was lonely. I had read too many books and hadn't made any friends.

She said she was lonely too, and that it had been hard to make friends. A lot of the people she'd met moved on, and that had taken its toll on her. "I'm not going anywhere for a while," I said.

And finally I started feeling sleepy. "Mar, I'm getting kind of tired. But I'm really glad we've met. Sorry if I've been running at the mouth, it's just been so hard to find people, you know?"

Mar's face drained of expression. She stared at me. Then she began to cry, no sound, just two steady streaks running down her cheeks and neck. She wiped her face with her fingers. "Oh, Christ, I'm sorry. I hardly know you, it's just, listen, I really don't want to be alone and have something happen and forget again. I tried to call my mom, but she was on vacation." She took a breath and looked out the dark window. "It's as if someone else is doing these things." I thought about how her insides were empty rooms by the sea, rocking when they shouldn't be, and I thought about those shapes rolling in on the surf. "I'm sorry," she said. "I'm really scared of being alone right now."

"Listen, it's late, why don't you sleep on my couch? Would that help?"

"That would be great," she said. "Thank you."

So that's what she did. I made Mar some chamomile tea because she said it might calm her. We sat together at my kitchen table and talked about quieter things than shapes in places they don't belong and misplaced people. The foghorns blew and we both remarked how comforting a sound that was for us. "This is a good apartment to listen to the rain," I said.

When we finished our tea I got her some blankets and a pillow for the couch, and I filled two mason jars with water, one for me and one for her. I turned off the kitchen light and put her mason jar on the table beside the couch. "Thank you," she said as I was crawling into bed. The voice without her face, deep and rough, floated around the living room into my room, wiped past the side of my face, until I said, "Sweet dreams."

"Fat chance," she said, and the voice rested beside me on my pillow, and I slept.

I spent all day Saturday with Mar. In the morning she tried to call a counselor she used to see at Clatsop Mental Health. She called her at home and left a message. She said she had gone into counseling when she first moved here because she was losing time, but that she had been doing pretty well since then, and her counselor had to take on new clients.

"After all," she reminded me, "Astoria does have the highest suicide rate in the country." She sipped on her coffee, steam rising into her face. "Alcoholism and domestic violence are pretty high up there too," she added.

"Thanks for the information," I said.

"And most clients don't refuse medication," she said. "You refuse anti-psychotics and they think they can't do anything for you." We were sitting at the kitchen table. "Would you want to take anti-psychotics?"

"No," I said, glancing at a paintbrush on my counter as if it was foreign. Perhaps I should have cited situations in which medication might make a difference, but I didn't. Truth was, I might have refused it too.

Mar tried her parents again, and again she left a message. "Still on vacation," she said. "They're always on vacation."

Later we walked down the railroad tracks from my place and into town for a good greasy breakfast. Mar said she didn't know how much she could stomach, but she'd give it her best shot. We stepped over some syringes in the grass.

"Christ," I said. "This shit really scares me."

Mar didn't say anything. Pilings poked out of the water. "People used to work there. Everyday, canning things, shelling things, filleting, right there where there's nothing. Imagine," she said finally. Seals barked under the tracks, their rough voices echoing as if through a tunnel.

An old man, sunlight on his face, said, "Hey, hi there." He rushed at Mar, his hand out, the top half of his body moving ahead of the rest of him. Mar stepped out of his way. "Christ!" she said, surprised. Instead of making contact with her—shaking her hand, patting her back, putting his arm around her, knocking her down, who knows—he stumbled and nearly fell face forward in the gravel. He looked back at her, glaring, confused, betrayed. He grumbled something, and inside me the grumble echoed like one of those dreams where you're trying to tell someone something but you can't speak and instead make frantic guttural sounds. Then he stumbled off in the other direction.

"You know him?" I said to Mar.

"No. I mean, no." She turned to watch him go then winked at me. "Unless of course I met him and forgot." We didn't talk for a long while.

Late in the afternoon Mar suggested we have a campfire on the beach. We drove to the store for beer and hot dogs. We went to the same beach where I'd met her the day before. I gathered wood, and Mar made the fire. The sun went down as we thrust our hot dog sticks over the flames. When it got chillier, she put on the sweater I'd given her.

The sky turned dark, and Mar took a walk down the beach. I lay on my back staring up at the stars. I thought about what it would be like to have Mar lying next to me. My little apartment, my books, all seemed far away. It was as if someone had cut a string that tied me there, and I wasn't able to reconnect it. Sometimes comfort can be a disconcerting thing, unsettling. I thought about the smell of my own sheets, how they felt cool against my body, how the top sheet folded over the edge of the comforter. How the foghorns blew at night. Instead, above me was an enormous sky and stars so far away.

"Robin, Robin," Mar called. "Come here. There's bioluminescence."

I sat up. "What?"

"In the water, sparks. It's neat."

Mar was standing above me just within the circle of firelight, her face only half lit. "Want to go down and see?"

"Sure," I said.

We walked down to the shore together, the little light getting farther away. I wondered, when I heard the surf up close, if I'd see those shapes Mar had drawn all lit up, rolling in.

"Stomp your feet," Mar said as she danced on top of the sand. Sparks flew in all directions. Mar started screaming and hollering and leaping in circles, and I did the same beside her. Then we stopped out of breath and collapsed onto the sand. We stared at each other a long time not speaking.

"Do you want to stay here tonight?" Mar asked.

"All right," I said slowly.

"I saw a sleeping bag in your truck," Mar said. "We could start a fire in one of those huts, get out of the wind, keep the fire low, let the coals warm us."

"All right," I said, again thinking about my cool white sheets and the smell of my pillow.

Mar got the fire going in the very same hut I had been in the day before. There was just enough room for both of us, the fire, and the table with the flakes of red. Mar liked the table and didn't want to move it, even though it would have given us more room. I unzipped the sleeping bag all the way so it was one big square. Then I lay down and curled on my side and watched Mar mess with the fire. My face felt warm. Mar took off her sweater and curled it up into a pillow. She lay beside me also on her side facing the fire. She pulled the other half of the sleeping bag over us. I put my arm around her and kissed her ear. We listened to the surf.

Mar's voice, lower and quieter than usual, floated in the dimness above us. "Once I was reading a book and I came across the word, 'mar.' I must have been, oh, maybe twelve. I looked it up in the dictionary because until then I had always thought mar was the sea. But the dictionary said, 'to damage or deface.' Then it said, 'a mark that disfigures.' I wrote that one down. Seems like of all the things I've forgotten, I never forgot that."

"Mar's the sea in Spanish," I said because the waves sounded so nice and because the shapes she'd drawn were cutting at my insides and I didn't want to hear any more.

"Robin, I woke up one morning, not even a week ago, and there were holes in my arms, a bunch of holes. And a few days before that I woke up here, in this hut, covered in vomit. I don't even know how much time I've missed. I swear I don't remember making the holes. I know it sounds crazy, but you needed to know." I was quiet. "There's something really horrible inside me; somebody's screaming." Once I read in a textbook that babies cry in the womb.

I closed my eyes and rested my arm long ways on top of Mar's arm, pressed my hand over hers and squeezed. I stroked her arms through her white T-shirt and kissed her shoulder, resting my chin there awhile. Quicker than I would have expected, she was asleep. I lay awake a long time unable to make the discomfort inside go away. Finally I counted down from a hundred and lost count sometime before thirty.

⸻ ⟋⟍ ⸻

I rolled over to hold Mar again, but she was gone. The fire had gone out. Reaching in the dark for the flashlight, I found it, too, was gone. I felt panicky, scared. It was so dark. I crouched beside the table and rested my elbows on it. I couldn't see the table or the walls. Light comprised of a compression of stars shone through the driftwood knots and pinpointed the white insides of my arms. I couldn't see my hands clasped together.

I removed my arms from the table and knelt on the ground. With my palms in the sand, I searched for the rocks around the fire. Then I felt for the table, and crawled between the two so I didn't burn myself.

Outside the hut the sky was filled with millions of stars, so many stars they frightened me. They just wouldn't stop. My heart beat in every part of my body. I had to find Mar. I knew the beach and easily found the dunes trail. The dune grasses rustled in the wind. I walked quickly, my heart in my mouth. In the parking lot I nearly screamed for the darkness and the emptiness. But then there, there was my truck. I fumbled with the key. It scratched against the door until it found the hole. I leapt in the truck, turned on the light, took many long breaths, put my hand to my heart. I opened the window to the back, called, "Mar?" quietly, questioning. But, of course, no answer. I drove out of the parking lot.

I drove all the way into town before I saw Mar. I noticed the little white triangle where the buttons of my sweater revealed her T-shirt. She was almost to the Portway and had just turned off the road and was headed for the railroad tracks. I parked my truck in the Portway parking lot, and by the time I got out, she had disappeared again. I walked quickly toward the tracks. Voices and smoke rose out of the night from down by the river.

From the cluster of sound I heard, "Hi, Honey. We was just talkin' about you."

At first I couldn't tell exactly where the voices were coming from. Blackberries separated me from the smoke. Ducking my head, I pushed the blackberries aside with my arm; they poked into my skin.

I was standing on rocks overlooking a small beach and a campfire surrounded by old bent heads, as if I were in the upper right-hand corner of a photograph. Mar, with a needle in her arm, turned and looked up at me.

"What are you looking at?" the man I had met earlier asked Mar. I saw the dark side of his face now, the fire accentuating the places where it had sunk into itself. I looked up the bank and into the empty night. For a moment I saw myself, the me who'd driven into town from Kansas, her head filled with a sky crowded with birds, staring through the glass in astonishment as the world changed from brown wheat fields to daffodil fields to ocean. It was the clean me, the me with a home, with no bruises and no holes.

Festival

Baby Michelle slept like a kitten against Sheila's chest, Nick's white crew hat completely covering her face so it was hard to tell she was anything other than part of the baby sack. Nick lifted the edge of the hat with his thumb, but all he saw was the hat's arcing shadow; even her tiny red fists had disappeared into folds of cloth. "Hey there, Little Buddy."

"Stop calling her that," Sheila said.

The air smelled of butter and corn and meat, and the cacophony of twenty or so bands playing at once stirred Nick, the rhythm like a pulse. He wanted to jump up and down in a crowd close to the stage and the speakers which thumped like his insides thumped, to hold his arms in the air and shout above the deafening sounds of a grunge or punk band, to bash his body against the bodies of others.

"But that's my Gilligan hat," Nick said, stepping in place so as not to get ahead of Sheila. He'd gotten the hat on a trip to the coast to visit his aunt and uncle. They were always giving him gifts. As a child he'd loved them more than he'd loved his own parents, a love that eventually turned to shame the more he grew to dislike his parents. He'd grabbed the hat along with the one small duffle bag of stuff he cared anything about—his coolest shirts and surfer shorts, some books Sheila'd given him, and a couple of giant moonshells—when his parents had "recommended" he move out. "We just can't take it," his mother'd said, meaning, *we don't want to be responsible for your baby.* He should have been glad his life with them was over, but instead he'd hated himself for not leaving sooner, hated himself for waiting until he'd gotten his high school girlfriend pregnant and moved out only by default.

"Hey, Gilligan," Nick said to the hat.

"She's a girl."

A clown man on stilts, his face divided into four squares, each painted black or white, stalked toward them, three small children running around his wooden legs.

"I bet he falls," Nick said.

"I need to sit down." Sheila stopped and waved her hand in front of her red face.

One of the children grabbed at the clown's pant leg, and the clown struck the child in the side. Stunned, the child backed away, holding one arm against the spot, shocked perhaps by the solidness of the leg inside those airy, spotted pants.

"But Super Deluxe—"

Sheila wandered off the sidewalk and into the shade of a tree. Nick followed and stood over her as she lifted Baby Michelle out of the sack and drew her up toward her shoulder. The baby bag hung off his shoulder as if it were a new appendage to his body. The baby's mouth was opening and closing and her arms were bent up toward her face, her fists slightly clenching and unclenching. She was like someone's science project, a larvae with eyes shut tight. "She's hungry."

"How can you tell?" He heard a far away crowd screaming and clapping, and he knew Super Deluxe had just been introduced in the outside arena. Sheila opened her shirt, and Baby Michelle latched onto her breast—it was like something out of the Animal

Kingdom. Nick looked behind him, at the path to the outside arena. Some people were walking fast and others were running. He stood with his hands in his pockets.

"Nick," Sheila said.

"Yeah?"

"I'm tired."

He looked away from the suckling at the trampled grass, at a corndog stick and a paper plate. The ground hummed with the sound of an electric bass—Super Deluxe. If he answered her, she might want to go back to the studio, and that was the last thing he wanted, to spend another day in the hot studio while Michelle and Sheila slept on the mattress, or walk aimlessly around Pioneer Square with no cash, bumming cigarettes from the junkies in the park, and finally coming home to Sheila and Michelle, their faces red and glistening with sweat. Or, if he were lucky, he could sit on the curb smoking with Rusty and Madrella and laughing as Madrella chastised people on the street: "Get a life, man," she'd said to a guy whose spotted dog wore a bandana and a harmonica around its neck while the guy shook a can of change.

"Why won't you just sit down?" Sheila asked.

But he couldn't sit down. He watched a boy, waist high, playing "Dust My Broom" on a small metal guitar; a woman in a long paisley skirt dropped a dollar in his open guitar case.

"Can I get you something?" he asked, thinking he was supposed to do something. After all, he was the father, though this fact didn't make him feel any different than he'd felt three months ago before Michelle was born, except that he no longer lived at home. Home was a funny word. To some people, he supposed, it meant a place where two people could raise a child—toys buried in the backyard, coins hidden behind the radiator, a window filled with a giant oak branch, the sound of lawnmowers on the weekends, and the smell of fresh cut grass; maybe for others a cabin in the woods with a sturdy front porch and curling black and white photos of generations of children tacked to the walls and a neatly stacked woodpile outside covered with a blue tarp. But home had never been any of these things, not for him, and not for Sheila.

For Nick home had been one tiny square house after another, cardboard houses, he called them, the early ones on the south side of Seattle nailed together when Boeing had first come to the city promising jobs for all. This "promise" was lost on his father who'd long been laid off and hadn't been able to hold down work nearly all of Nick's life so that each year his parents moved further and further out: Federal Way, SeaTac, White Center. For Sheila home had been crappy apartments her mom kept losing—she'd grown too old for the temporary labor pool. Even if Nick could hope for some sort of home in the future, he couldn't actually imagine it. What he knew of home now was a mattress on the floor of a friend's art studio, although it wasn't actually an art studio—there was no artist. It was a place he and Sheila and the baby and his so-called friends Rusty and Madrella could stay for cheap, and it wasn't like it was permanent.

"Just sit down," Sheila said.

"How about some corn?"

"We're broke, Nick."

"It's only two dollars."

"Stop it." Sheila tried to pull Baby Michelle off her nipple. "She's got some strong gums." But Michelle dug her hands into Sheila's chest and hung on tight with her tiny mouth.

"You want something to drink?"

"Do what you want," Sheila said.

He fingered the bus change in his pocket and clasped and unclasped the single key that opened the studio. "It's worse at home," he said finally. "Don't you want to see Super Deluxe, Sheila?"

Michelle shook herself loose from Sheila's breast, and Sheila held her against her shoulder and patted her back until she belched. A woman in a tie-dyed skirt and white T-shirt was painting a vine of flowers on a small girl's arm. When she finished, she pulled out a tube and sprinkled sparkles on the wet paint. The girl, white blonde hair falling across her forehead and into one eye, examined the arm. "I like it," she said finally. He tried to imagine Baby Michelle turning into this girl, but could not. She was a mole with x's over its eyes, a kitten still slick with the wet from its mother's uterus.

The first night back from the hospital, he'd lain on his back, Michelle sleeping in the curving space below his collarbone. When he closed his eyes, he couldn't tell the difference between Michelle and Mittens, the family cat who used to curl up on his chest and purr. He'd listened to the whir of the window fan and felt the heavy weight of boredom.

"These tickets are really expensive," Nick said. His friend Kyle had given them the tickets to Bumbershoot because he had to go to his grandmother's funeral in Massachusetts. "We're really lucky to have them. Kyle'd be bummed if we just left."

"I didn't say anything," Sheila said.

"Okay, I know. Sorry."

Last year Nick and Sheila had gone to Bumbershoot together, and the year before that, and the year before that, and even, he thinks, the year before that. Some years they'd gone as friends, and then they'd gone as boyfriend and girlfriend, and then they'd gone knowing. Last summer they'd sat on the edge of the giant fountain, an upside-down cement dome as big as a basketball court where water sprayed out of thousands of holes. In the day time, kids ran around it as if through a giant sprinkler, and at night teenagers hung out around the edges. Nick and Sheila had run through the water and soaked their clothes then sat on the cement lip and he'd gotten stoned. Sheila's thin lips, purplish from the cold, quivered, and Nick held her against his wet body. She said, "I do believe in a woman's right to choose, and I choose a baby." He'd loved her then, as much as a new high school graduate could love the girl who'd been his best friend for years.

Now he wondered as he watched her long, tight face rimmed with sweat. She was wearing his polka dotted button-up shirt because she didn't have any button ups. Sheila wore mostly tight shirts with frills on the edges and denim skirts. He'd always thought her sense of style was so awful it was charming. His friends, though, hadn't found it so charming. "Frumpy," Rusty had said when Nick first told him he and Sheila were going out. That broke everyone up—who says "frumpy"? "She's gonna drag you down, man," Rusty had said. "You're gonna be hanging out around the high school like some letch when you graduate and she's still finishing up." And when he brought Sheila around his friends, he could see them close up, shut him out. Except for Kyle. Kyle thought Sheila was alright. He didn't care if she didn't have any friends besides Nick, if she had bad acne and liked Medieval role playing. "It's all different in college," Kyle'd said. "Smart girls like Sheila get to be cool." Maybe that was true, he thought now, but any ideas about college had disappeared a year ago. Not that Nick had any real ideas about college, although now it sounded like some great escape.

"I got an idea," Nick said.

"Great." Sheila'd mastered sarcasm quickly, a wit that had been foreign to her until she started hanging around Nick.

"No really, Sheil, you'll like it. We could go back by the art rooms and hang out by the wading pool with the rocks. There's a stage back there, so we could listen to music and you and Gilligan—"

"Stop it, Nick." Her voice quivered.

Nick withdrew. "Michelle, could hang out in the shade. You could put your feet in the water."

"Fine," she said. "Just don't walk so fast, okay?"

"Sure, Sheil." He wished she'd acknowledge the fact that he'd given up the Super Deluxe concert; instead, she got up slowly, as if she were following him for his sake, as if he wanted to hang out by the kiddie wading pool. "You could check out the art rooms and the book fair."

"I said okay."

In the hour they'd been there, the crowds had gotten increasingly thicker, and walking took most of his concentration. Nick pushed ahead, as if parting the crowd for Michelle and Sheila, but more often than not, the crowd closed up after him, and next time he'd look back, Sheila would be lost. Passing a four-way intersection, food vendors in all directions, was the toughest, but Nick moved through the crowds like an expert child, sliding his body sideways and pressing around people as if he had someplace important to be, refusing to be caught still among them all. It was a game with him, how quickly could he move? Soon he was touching old ladies on the back, 'scuse me, 'scuse me, winding his way out of the intersection and up the wide steps away from the food vendors and the center of the park, through a crowd circling a mime, and into one of the back corners of the festival.

By the time he got to the wading pools, he'd lost Sheila completely. He claimed a shady spot at the end of the pool and against a wall from which a small waterfall fell. Large rocks were strewn about the pool. A toddler in red shorts waded in the knee-deep white-green water, and a little girl in a Big Bird bathing suit sat on a rock, her hair slicked back with water, her knees drawn up into her body. Nick looked down the outdoor corridor lined with vendors selling jewelry and flowing patterned skirts and wooden instruments from Eastern countries. The air smelled of incense. The crowd, still at least ten people wide, snaked out like a forked tongue into the masses of people pressing up against the food vendors he'd just left. Sheila was in there somewhere. He searched for Michelle's white cap, for Sheila's polka dotted shirt but could see neither. He stood up on the edge of the pool and looked over the tops of the heads and finally spotted the little white Gilligan cap as if it were a hat on a doll pressed against Sheila's stomach. Sheila's head was down; she was moving slower than the people around her. Two young girls pushed past her, and a boy in shorts came after as if chasing them. Nick hopped down from the rim of the pool and pushed through the crowd toward her.

"Here," she said, when he got close. "Take her," and she thrust Michelle into his arms. "Keep her head out of the sun. She's still sleeping."

Nick couldn't see Michelle's face, but when he rested her against his shoulder, her hands instinctively clutched the cotton of his T-shirt, and her cheek fell neatly into the cup of his shoulder. She felt heavy and hot. "Over here. There's an empty spot in the shade right near the rock waterfall."

"Fine," Sheila said.

"It's a great spot, Sheil."

"I believe you."

"We're lucky no one's taken it," he said when they got back to the spot by the waterfall. The shadows of leaves formed squiggly lattices on the pool's shallow bottom and spotted the cement edge. Spray from the waterfall clung to Sheila's pale, unshaven legs. Michelle tried to lift her head, and Nick supported it with his palm. But before she even opened her eyes, she began to wail, her face rapidly turning bright red, and he was reminded of a Jane Goodall film he saw in grade school of gorillas being born. What helpless, hairless little blobs, he'd thought, though Jane Goodall fondly compared them to human children. Even Michelle's neck was bright red, her eyes pinched shut. The scream reverberated inside him, striking his pulse like a flair of panic. He looked helplessly at Sheila who held out her arms.

A woman folksinger was playing on the stage behind them, and there was a long line to get into the beer garden. Nick didn't want to even try, though the thought had crossed his mind more than once. Michelle's screaming rattled inside his head; it made him feel so weary, it might as well have been three o'clock in the morning and still deadly hot in the studio, Nick curled up on the mattress, naked and sweaty despite the window fan, watching Sheila pace around the mattress because there was nowhere else to go. He'd glance at Rusty and Madrella, Rusty always dramatically covering his head with a pillow. Madrella would eventually get up and stomp to the bathroom or get a glass of water, as if to make sure they knew Michelle had woken her. He'd lie awake the rest of the night wondering what they'd do if they were kicked out; then he'd worry about work. The restaurant had cut back his hours, and he couldn't find the time to search for another job. He'd bummed around Pike Place Market asking friends, but nobody had anything that would pay as much as the restaurant or that would work around his hours. He'd lay awake at night listening to the occasional outbursts of arguments in the streets, watching the lights of cars on the wall of the building across the street through the studio's grimy windows, panicked inside; still, the extent to which things had to change, not by default but by intention, hadn't yet completely occurred to him.

Sheila walked slowly back and forth while Nick sat on the edge of the pool, his elbows over his knees, his chin in his hands, and watched. Her palm moved in slow circles across Michelle's back while Michelle choked into her shoulder. It was early evening, and even though the sun was still hot, soon it would sink below the perimeters of the park, and night would descend on the festival; people would be twirling glow sticks and dancing barefoot. The Space Needle would be lit up, and the Ferris Wheel lights would circle like stars. Maybe he could still catch the drum circle. A drunk woman clung to a tattooed man, and a dog on a rope rested his nose on the cement behind a booth selling tie dyes.

"Nick, the bag. I need a diaper."

"Oh, sorry." He stood up and took the bag off his shoulder and began to rifle through it.

"The quilt, I need that too."

"Here's the diaper."

"I need the quilt first."

But when Nick couldn't find it right away, Sheila pulled the bag away from him, Michelle weeping into her other shoulder, and, without even looking, pulled out the thick baby quilt his aunt and uncle had given them. It was one of the few generous gestures anyone had made since Sheila had gotten pregnant. It came with a $100 bill and a plea to bring the baby for a visit. But Nick put the money toward rent—Sheila'd held it momentarily, as if she'd wanted to object. She'd only met his aunt and uncle once, when they'd visited Seattle, before Nick and Sheila were even dating. Sheila and his aunt had launched into a long discussion of *The Once and Future King*, a book Nick, at 15, had had no interest in, although admittedly the fact that Sheila had carried around such a fat, dog-eared book had been one of the things that had impressed him about her. Sheila was the realistic one—even if she had wanted to go visit the coast, she wouldn't have said so. Instead, she'd stared wistfully at the bill. As for Nick, visiting his aunt and uncle in Port Angeles had ceased to be an escape hatch years ago. After all, he'd grown up and spent less and less time at home and more and more time exploring the city with his friends—it was too late to be rescued. His aunt and uncle had called regularly over the past five years inviting him to visit, but there was always a concert he'd miss, a club opening he had to be at, or a party.

The last time he'd visited, he'd spent most of his time sneaking around so he could get stoned. He'd wander up and down the shore staring at the slow and rhythmic waves thinning on the sand, wind echoing in his inner ear as if there were no other sounds. He could see the disappointment in their faces when he hadn't been back on time for his aunt's dinners—dinners in the past he'd relished, Northwest dishes with wild mushrooms and venison and mussels. Fresh vegetables from their garden. They must have known he was stoned, and he suspected they saw him just as his parents saw him—trouble.

"Sorry," he said as Sheila handed him the quilt.

"It's fine. Lay it out."

He spread the quilt across the cement, and Sheila lay Michelle on her back. She grew instantly still, surprisingly accustomed to the routine.

"She's gotten really good at this," Sheila said.

"That's my Gilligan."

This time, Sheila didn't even look up.

He stood awkwardly over the two of them, watching a patch of light slip across Michelle's leg.

"It's okay, Nick, you can go check things out if you want. We're fine here."

"I can stay."

"You're making me nervous," Sheila said as she taped the last Pamper wing to the front.

"Oh." Since when had she become the boss? He shuffled away from them, his hands in his pockets, then turned back for a moment. "I won't be gone long."

"Take as long as you want." She dipped a hand into the water and wet the edges of Michelle's face and neck then turned her over on her stomach on the quilt. A boy in cutoffs stood up on the cement ledge behind Sheila and shouted, "You little whore!" and a tank-topped girl with glitter on her eyes screamed back from the other side of the pool, "Fuck you, asshole!"

"See you, Sheil," Nick said weakly, but she didn't seem to hear him.

He knew he should stay close, so he wandered through the book fair, browsed at the comic book tables and the zine tables.

He watched five film shorts, but when he walked out, he couldn't recall what they'd been about. In the first art room was a display of slashed and bloody Barbie dolls encased in a mixture of glass and wooden boxes. In one, Ken was raping Barbie with a white plastic picnic knife. So what, he thought, and left.

The next room was so dark Nick felt suddenly thrust into a blind world. He walked slowly, his palms behind his back touching a black curtain that helped the room seem as if it had no end, as if it were some infinity in space, except for five circles of color projected onto one wall. He couldn't see the projector. The circles were cut with lines and seemed to open and close like geometric representations of eyes. They spun and moved to the rhythms of atonal noise, the computerized plucking of strings, percussive and irregular, like the sounds in a German industrial club. Nick, being drawn to industrial noise and easily hypnotized, sunk into a corner and watched. The shapes floated in a darkness so visceral, even the outlines of people sitting on the floor around him or leaning against the wall were hard to make out, and he was so drawn to the shapes, that he didn't even try to see them. He stared at the spinning circles, jolting and stopping and spinning again, opening and closing; he saw them multiply such that if he looked away, a new one would appear momentarily hanging in the blackness and then disappear. His breathing slowed so that his entire body became aware of the breathing. And then everything fell away from him; he had no girlfriend, no child, no parents, no life. Even his body lost its tightness and floated away from him. There was a new space inside him, a dark, quiet space where he could lay his mind, take off his shoes, forget the crashing impossibility of getting through everyday, the heavy boredom, the worry, the building fear: in pushing away from their parents they'd ended up worse off. He breathed this knowledge out of him. It was as if for months he'd simply forgotten to breathe. And now the sound of his breathing synchronized itself with the spinning of the circles and the off-kilter pinging of atonal rhythm. When he closed his eyes, he saw the discs as if forever after he'd see those discs every time he took a deep breath and looked inside himself, and he'd feel comforted by that.

When he stepped out, blinking and floaty, the sun had gone down, and a thin moon hung in the darkening sky. A jazz band with a crazy electric bassist played discordant music on the stage where the folk singer had been, and smoke from smokers in the beer garden rose in shafts of light. Sheila was leaning against the wall, the baby bag supporting the small of her back. Her shoes were off, and Michelle rested against her shoulder. For a moment, Nick imagined a different world: they live in a cabin on the Olympic Peninsula, and in the daytime, Sheila and Michelle sit by a mossy waterfall, Sheila occasionally diving into a bright green pool while Michelle sleeps on her stomach on a mossy bank. Nick, having just split wood for the woodstove, stands at a distance, watching them, enamored and at home. Behind Sheila's peaceful face he heard the tinkling of the waterfall; he pictured a little red bed for Michelle in their cabin, and the stars at night forming a wide belt of light across the sky cut only by the jagged tops of cedar and fir and hemlock. All of this he saw in her sleeping face.

"Sheil?" he whispered finally. Far off, he could hear Bumbershoot's nighttime drum circle. It was like a pulse beneath the jazz band and the busy chattering of the people.

Sheila's eyes fluttered open, and she stared at him a moment, as if waking up from a dream. "Where am I?"

He sat down and rested his chin on her knees which were drawn up toward her body.

"She's sucking her thumb," Nick whispered. Just like the baby gorillas.

"Can we go home?" Sheila asked. Her face seemed to change, from the peace of sleep to an expression of veiled angst that was new to him, either because he was seeing it for the first time, though it may have been there all along, or because she was closer to the point of breaking than he had otherwise suspected.

"You okay?"

"Sure," she said. "It's just, my shoulder hurts."

Nick took Michelle as Sheila put on her plastic jelly shoes. Then she took Michelle back, and he took the bag, as usual. The crowds had thinned. Sheila didn't speak to him. They passed a juggler and a clown, the clown wandering precariously under the juggler's bowling pins, then squeaking a hand-held horn and acting like he hadn't noticed how close he'd come to being knocked out. A woman in a tank top, her eyes red from crying, stood and watched shyly, and a fat man paused, bit the top off a corndog, and walked on.

"Got a cigarette?" asked a magician sitting on a low cement ledge, his legs crossed at the knees, his hat crumpled. He looked drunk and mean.

"Sorry, man," Nick said. "Just out." Which was true. He hadn't had a cigarette for hours, which made it easier for him to think about going home. There was at least an old dried up package of Drum in the studio, if Rusty hadn't gotten to it.

A giant dragon on the back of five unicyclists snaked down the sidewalk past the food booths. Nick held Sheila's arm, and they stepped aside and watched the blind unicyclists pedal by, silver spots like mirrors along the dragon's side reflecting the lights of concession stands. A reggae band played and the sound merged with the sound of drumming, which got louder the closer they got to the exit. Papier mâché monsters hung on sticks beside a small acrobatic stage where a woman spun horizontally in circles on a man's back, and a ringmaster clapped from the wings.

They were walking straight toward the drumming circle. Nick gazed at the silhouettes of twenty or thirty people leaning over their drums and imagined their pulses jumping out of their crazy rhythms and steadying, pressing away the rest of the world with their collective beat. They turned at the corn stand, passed the Bagley Wright Theatre, and passed the boy who was still playing "Dust My Broom." Just looking at him made Nick weary. A man at the gate asked to stamp their hands; Sheila said no, but Nick held his out.

"We can't go back," Sheila said.

"I know, I just," but he didn't have an answer for her. He just wanted to? Wanted to what? Send his girlfriend and child home on a bus alone so he could go back and join the drum circle? Or hang out around the beer gardens he couldn't get into?

"Nicky!" Rusty stood wavering on the curb, his face deep red with sunburn and alcohol. "What's up man? Y'all goin' home?"

Madrella was selling "fresh" raspberry lemonade, a favorite scam of hers where she mixed Kool-Aid into cups then acted like she'd made it herself. The plastic cups were lined up on a cardboard box. "Hand squeezed today!" she called out to passersby.

"Sheila's beat," Nick said and immediately regretted blaming her. But then, Sheila seemed to have given up on him and was walking slowly down the street toward the bus stop. Fuck her. He felt like the mean magician in desperate need of a cigarette. "You got a smoke?"

"No way, man. We got one left between the two of us."

A couple walked by, and the woman glanced at Madrella's drinks briefly.

"Fresh squeezed!"

The woman quickly looked away, as if trying not to be sold something.

"Fuck you!" Madrella screamed, and Rusty laughed, the light falling across his face turning him into a creepy clown.

"Fuck you too!" she yelled at Rusty.

Maybe Nick should laugh too, but inside him was a space of silence, and that silence had a new protectiveness; it pressed Madrella and Rusty out. He felt a deep sense of shame, and that's when he saw Sheila crossing the road in front of the offended couple. He pushed the baby bag further up on his shoulder and ran toward her.

Sheila was slumped against the wall of a cement office building next to the bus stop. From far off, she looked like a bag lady, Michelle and the baby sack just another layer of junk covering her body. When he reached her, she was crying. He took Michelle out of her arms, and Sheila leaned forward draping her arms over her knees and bawled at the ground, which smelled of dust and cigarette butts and piss. Michelle's arms and legs flailed about as if she were blind and lost until they settled on his chest.

"Sheila?" He bent beside her.

"I'll never go to college," she said finally through tears. "I can't do this. I didn't know it would be so hard. I really wanted to go to school." She held her hands up to her face as if embarrassed by her tears.

"You'll go, Sheil. You're the smart one, remember?"

She looked into his face, and he could see that the earlier angst had turned to panic had turned to fear had turned to vulnerability. "I'll never go."

"We'll figure something out," he said.

"We don't have any money."

"I can try harder to get work," he said.

"It won't be enough," Sheila said, rubbing her eyes with the base of her fist. But the tears leaked out the edges of her eyes still.

Michelle's fists grabbed Nick's shirt as she adjusted her head on his shoulder. He felt the shirt pulling across his chest. The baby bag still hung off his other shoulder.

"Maybe we could talk to my uncle in Port Angeles. There's a community college there."

Sheila studied him carefully. She wiped her face with her sleeve. "You'd talk to them? Even though we spent their money on rent?"

This was not an option Nick had considered until now. And there was no way of knowing whether it really was an option, but then deliberate change hadn't seemed an option until now. Until now, Nick had spent his life waiting to see what would happen next: would his father lose his job again? How blasted would he get? Would he even come home? Where would the family move next? Nothing he had done, like comforting his mother when she wept, had made a difference, and so he'd waited. Until now, he couldn't imagine the thought of leaving his friends, of not being king of the city he grew up in, not having the clubs or the festivals or the concerts, not following the rush of every moment's beat as if devouring every moment were about pushing the past and the future further away. But watching Sheila slumped against the grimy stone of some anonymous office building surrounded by the smell of exhaust and the far away sharp laughter of drunks piling in and out of bars surrounding the festival, it seemed to him that something he couldn't imagine might be exactly what was necessary.

"They like you, Sheil," he said finally.

"You'd leave Seattle?"

"Sure," he said. "I'm not saying it'll work, but we could try." He thought of the quiet curve of Sequim Spit, the way the wind in his ears made sound disappear and the perfect discs of sand dollars and the spiraling circles of moonshells he'd found there.

The bus pulled up, and Nick helped Sheila off the ground. She took the bag, he put his arm around her, and as they stood in line, she rested her head against his shoulder just as she had when she'd been pregnant, that hopeful night they'd watched drops of water shoot into the air and disappear. She had not completely stopped crying, but at least they were on their way home.

The bus sighed as the door squealed shut. The floor moved beneath him. Sheila leaned her face against the window. Her sobbing stopped, and soon her head fell back, and he could hear her deep sleep breathing. Michelle lifted her head, and he supported it with his hand. "Hey there, little buddy," he whispered, taking off the hat. She looked up into his eyes, perhaps fully for the first time, and stared at him as if she had never actually seen him before. She didn't blink, even as the city lights passed across her tiny face. It was as if she were hypnotized by him and he by her. He imagined they were playing a game of who can stare the longest when quite suddenly he saw a person looking back at him, gazing into his eyes, curious and trusting and open.

How to Make an Island

Edith is leaving. Her friends are having a party for her on a boat. She invited me because we're always together and because she's scared of boats. She said she'd feel safe if I was with her. All around us is gray water and gray air. Fog moves among the coastal mountains. In the distance are low islands.

I haven't been on a boat in many years. I like the rise and fall, the openness. The rocking makes Edith a little sick, but she covers it up well. Her left hand, hidden behind her back, grasps the low edge of the boat. There are a few things in this world I forever return to. The rock of a boat on water, the smell of salt and air, the noise of waves against something hollow. And a few forbidden places where I take shelter. Like Edith. Like Cayo Pelau.

—\\\\—

When I was twelve, my best friend Mac and I had planned a boat trip to the pirate island Cayo Pelau. It was cursed. My parents didn't want me sailing that far, but my father was going away, and Mac was staying at my house while he was gone. My father was going to the hospital to be with my mother. Then he was going to bring her home. I didn't know exactly what they were doing to

123

my mom. I didn't really want to know. But that she was dying was clear. And that she was coming home to die was certain.

Mac's real name was Maxine. I'd tease her about it, but she was much bigger than me, so I had to be careful. I had told Mac all the stories I knew about local pirates. In school we'd draw maps. I nabbed my father's boat charts, and we copied everything we needed to know on graph paper. We had ideas about islands.

—⁓—

Jose Gaspar supplied his men with an island to play on between battles with other ships. In the evenings there were bonfires. And women. Tobacco. Liquor. The doors of temporary houses opened just above the tide line. The legs of mangroves rose above them, air filtering through in long hot strips.

—⁓—

I press my face against the wind and think of things that leave, boats, trains, faces. And Edith. I call the boat a mullet boat because I am far from home. Home is a long strip of bleach, a beach and some sun. And islands. Where I'm from islands begin with a seed the shape of a slice of moon. Sand collects around the mangrove roots as it might around the legs of spider crabs and gathers land.

Where I live now is an archipelago of low gray mountains and islands near the mouth of a wide river. The air is dusty gray from constant rain. I am in the bow of a boat I call a mullet boat but isn't, a large, gutted wooden boat with a wide beam low to the water and a large console towards the stern. A handful of people are sitting on low seats or standing up for a look around, some with wine. I ask the man who keeps the boat beside his house, what kind of fish this boat is made to bring in. He says something inaudible about Alaska and proceeds with a list of fish, the names of which confuse me. Some of the names are familiar but do not represent the fish I know. I don't speak much after that.

Edith is speaking to everyone. She's holding the tiller and laughing, but I can see that she is sick to her stomach by the way she rocks against the waves. Her eyes occasionally look out to a steadier point. Layers of blues and grays, shadows without bodies.

———

Mac and I wrapped our clothes and supplies in black plastic trash bags. Early in the morning, the day after my father left, we bicycled to a remote spot of a marina, to a sailboat with one sail tied to an unsteady dock. The line was slack, the sky dark. I pulled the boat close to us so Mac could get on. Then I handed her the bags. We pulled out my father's weather reader and listened to the report before we untied. Small craft warning. We went anyway.

———

When I first met Edith I knew she would leave. She told me so. She tells me still. "I hate this place, Em."

———

"Emma. It's dark. What does that mean?" Mac said.

A flock of white pelicans perched among the deep green waxy leaves of a mangrove island. The sky was gray. The water was still.

———

Edith steers the boat close to land, where the water is calm. A man points to an eagle flying just above the trees. I can smell the land, dirt and trees. Unapproachable cliffs meet the gray water.

Edith is from the city. She wants to go back. She came here because she got offered a good job. But she knew it was a mistake, always. So now she's leaving. Third try, this one's for real.

A man with gray hair combed away from his face says to me, "I don't know you."

I say, "I'm Edith's friend."

"How come I haven't seen you around?"

I shrug and look towards Edith, her small face, but she doesn't see me.

"Can I get you some wine?" he asks.

"No thank you." He looks like older men I've known before. Right now I could be out on the water, standing somehow, looking back over my shoulder at the man and all the other people. Right now I feel as if Edith has already left, as if I could forget all the people I've ever really been close to.

—⁓—

The moment Mac and I passed the island with the white pelicans, the water opened up. Ahead our channel merged into the Intracoastal. The leeward deck dipped into the waves and water filled the cockpit. For moments Mac just stared at that water, not knowing quite what to do. Then she grabbed the bleach bucket with the cut-off top and began bailing. I let the main sheet out until the sail luffed, and the wind pushed us further off tack. More water poured over the side. Mac dropped the same water back into the Gulf.

When I tried to tack, the boat got stuck bow into the wind, the waves too big for it to pass through the wind and turn. So I jumped out, swam to the bow, and pushed it across the wind. Then I jumped back in. Mac was steadily bailing.

—⁓—

Edith has the tiller in her hand. The man who owns the boat is talking into her ear and pointing. We pass the edge of an island and the boat crosses an area of merging currents just beyond the point of land that juts out over the water. I'm leaning on a corner of the bow. I know that water has come up to the edge of my sleeve, but I don't feel it through the corduroy. Edith is looking straight at me when she lets go of the tiller and ducks beside the engine box. The tiller swings loose, but the owner of the boat grabs it back quickly. Some people laugh. Edith laughs too as she begins to stand again. But she's looking at me, and she's scared.

———※———

Mac dropped the bailer into the water, so I jumped out and grabbed it. Our bodies and the boat and the waves moved up and down for what seemed an hour or more. Fat swells lifted us high then the boat would drop fast, the bow pressing against the next wave, water splashing into the cockpit, all over Mac.

We were headed down the Intracoastal Waterway toward Boca Grande Pass. On the south side of the Pass was a series of islands, one of which was Cayo Pelau. Boca Grande Pass was too wide and deep for my little boat, but according to our charts, we could leave the Intracoastal and sail among the islands, avoiding the Pass altogether.

As soon as we could, we turned toward land. But the islands around us didn't match the ones we had drawn. We sailed in and among them until we saw a fisherman. His boat was still, his pole over the edge. He was an old man with a gray cap. We coasted by slowly, wind at our beam, sail only slightly filled. There were three islands around us. The water was shallow and Mac was lifting the centerboard up and down accordingly.

"Excuse me," I called out.

The fisherman looked up, pole steady, boat still.

"Which one is Cara Pelau?" That's what our charts said, Cara Pelau.

He lowered the pole and pushed his hat back, held one arm up and pointed. "That there is Cayo Pelau." The syllables came one at a time, cai-yo-pe-loo: a different name, the one the book said it was called when Gaspar's men played there.

―⁓〽⁓―

In the evenings there were bonfires. And women. The women slept on the floors of houses on stilts. The men left in the mornings. The women waited in the mangrove fanning themselves with their hands. The noises of men on boats drifted through the thick leaves, fading, then taken over by the buzz of mosquitoes in the heat.

―⁓〽⁓―

Edith wants to go back to the city. She says there's not enough to do here. Everywhere I look I am in love with the land, the blues and the grays, water and land and land and water. The sky is endless layers. You could follow the water to the mountains, and the mountains to further mountains, and the mountains to the sky, layers of clouds, another shade beyond that, islands of clouds, islands of mountains that look like clouds and clouds that look like islands.

Edith doesn't care much for islands. She likes music and street lights and crowds, buildings with red brick walls inside, high ceilings echoing with voices. I like staring out at the river from high on the hill, the bark of seals funneling up through the fog. Each day I see more islands. Nights Edith and I tell each other everything. I know, for example, boats make her sick to her stomach. She knows I don't hug, that when someone squeezes me, I don't squeeze back. She says she doesn't think I like contact at all.

Edith is sitting down in the stern near the console. The man who tried to talk to me has wandered into the group. I look away from the people. My eyes sting, and my face feels warm inside.

The tip of the peninsula is behind us now. Fog has covered the top of it, where the trees meet the sky.

———·៕——

We sailed around the north tip of Cayo Pelau. The fisherman and his aluminum boat disappeared as the mangroves of Cayo Pelau blocked off sight of the other islands. The water was rougher on the other side of the island. The wind was behind, the sail out, the bow occasionally dunking under the waves. Mac was hollering each time the bow went down. My skin felt hot in the new sun.

A large fish flipped out of the water and slid across the bow just in front of the cockpit. It brushed up against Mac's leg then flopped back into the green waves.

"Emma, see that?" Mac yelled against the sound of the waves.

"That there is Cai Yo Pe Loo!" I yelled back. There was a shadow of bright color left on the deck where the fish had been.

——៕——

Sometimes the men brought fish to the women. They stood over tables made of large wooden boat spools and cut them open, color spilling out and dropping onto the sand. Pelicans walked awkwardly through the mangroves carrying the heads. The women ate strips of raw fish.

——៕——

We coasted through shallow green water, white against the sides of the boat looking for a beach where we might be able to pull up.

"There must be something. How else could they have used this island, without a beach," I said.

Eventually the mangroves opened slightly to a small patch of white. This time I gave Mac the tiller and hopped off the bow. The ground was muddy beneath my tennis shoes. I pulled the bow onto the sand and Mac handed me the garbage bags. Together we pulled the boat as far as we could onto the beach and tied the painter to a mangrove branch. Large white and gray whelks, broken and spotted with age, were scattered among the mangrove roots.

We untied the bags and strung up a clothes line to hang our wet shorts and T-shirts. We had dry shirts, jeans, and snake boots in the bags. We had a knife, my father's weather reader, extra charts in clear plastic baggies, cheese, a loaf of bread, a jar of peanut butter, a handful of oranges, a gallon of water, one large red towel.

After we had put on our dry clothes and eaten, we went exploring. We followed what was possibly an old trail through the mangroves along the edge of the water.

"Where do you think they built the houses?" I asked.

"Maybe inside the island. You know, where it's drier," Mac said.

On one side of us was mangrove and water, and on the other side trees and palmetto brush. I climbed a tree to check if I could see any rooftops, anything besides the hot brush. Mac stood beneath me swatting at mosquitoes and looking up.

"It looks like the land rises there, dunes or something, maybe a clearing further off. I can't tell exactly," I said.

"I'm gonna keep walking," Mac said.

I climbed down and followed her.

Mac found a bottle like a whiskey flask. She pretended to drink it, and a foul-smelling liquid poured onto her face. I found a purple flower and stuffed it in the bottle. We put it down under the mangroves where the tide would carry it away.

"Let's go in there," I said. "Really Mac, I think there's a clearing. Maybe we'll find something."

"I don't think there's anything here," she said.

But I was already pushing my way through the brush, so she followed. The trees did open up which made it easier to walk. But there was no sign of houses, nothing except large sand mounds covered with grass and a few small trees. We played on the mounds, climbed up them, looking for some sign of the stories we knew. It was hot on the inside of the island. We couldn't imagine anyone living there. We took off our shirts.

———〰———

The Seminole Indians buried the dead with pieces of pottery, small animals carved out of wood, bits of plants, flowers and herbs, maybe a stone with a pattern on it. All these things they piled with the one who had died in huge mounds of sand reaching toward the sky.

———〰———

I lay down in the grass beneath a tree. Mac lay down behind me. I was quiet for a long time, Mac pressed up against me, her arm around me, my cheek resting against the ground.

"I can't imagine lying with a boy this way, being this close," Mac said after a while. I didn't really think about it.

"My mom's coming home to die," I said.

"God Emma," Mac pressed her cheek on top of mine. It felt warm with sun. "What are you going to do?" she said after a while.

"I don't know. Maybe read to her," I said.

"You could tell her stories," she said.

"About pirates that never existed?" I said. I hurt inside.

"No you fool. Tell her this story."

"About today?" I asked.

"About the bleach bucket bailer, how you swam after it," Mac said.

"And the fish that landed on our boat," I said.

"Yes, and the whelks,"

"the flower in the bottle,"

"these mounds," Mac said.

I got silent, my face pressed between Mac's cheek and the ground.

—⁓—

Edith and I are not lovers. She understands that better than I do because she is in love with a man in the city. Most of the time I understand too. But I must admit, sometimes I get confused.

I once loved a man who lived on an island. He had a beautiful face and hands like a woman's. Sometimes he'd hold my face between his palms. And other times he kept his hands in his pockets. I used to think love was distance. All my lovers were a distance of miles older than me.

Ahead of us, and coming up close, is an island which rises in the center. I cannot see the small town we live in from here. Behind this island are more islands. Each island is approximately five years of distance and only a mouthful of love. We move close to the island, and trace its borders in a sad, wide circle.

—⁓—

Mac and I capsized the boat just off the shore of Cayo Pelau. This, I was positive, was the curse. The bags disappeared. Mac tried to swim after them. They shouldn't have sunk, but they did. I thought about my mother, how I used to fall asleep with my head in her lap, how she smelled like hand lotion and wool, how she'd carry me to bed, myself weightless and cared for. I held the tiller and cried.

—⁓—

When I saw Mac a few years ago, she was with a large woman. When they held each other there was no space between their bodies. The island ahead of us is surrounded by gray space. I cannot tell what is water and what is air. Edith is looking out at the island, her face kind of curious but mostly sad. I used to think love was distance.

I wipe my face with my corduroy sleeve and make my way through the people. I sit on the wooden seat beside Edith, so close our legs are touching. I reach for her hand between our backs and squeeze it.

We circle the island and leave. I cannot be alone anymore.

Blue Plastic Shades

Fred's mother switched on his clown face lamp and leaned over him with a damp washcloth. He lay in his little red bed, afloat, sweating, a glass of water bluish on the bed stand. She folded the cloth in three parts and placed it across his forehead. "Take a sip of water, Freddy," she said and propped his pillows up behind him. He moved into a sitting position and held the glass between his hands. He stared up into her face, watching her closely as he drank, watching her as if that would make her stay. *I know a dark secluded place.* Fred opened his eyes. *Where no one knows your face.* Dusty's damp, silky ear lay across his cheek, and he was hugging her wiggling body against his chest. Muted morning light pushed against the grubby window; the clown lamp with its triangle eyebrows was turned off.

Dusty hadn't disappeared. Her wet tongue stroked his chin and nose and cheeks. *Hernando's Hideaway* played throughout the house, shook the domed walls and the tiny plywood paneled rooms. The ceiling over his head, low and made up of white water-stained squares, drooped around the light. The squares had tiny holes in them. He'd counted the squares. He'd counted the holes in a squares. He'd lost count. But this morning, all he wanted to do was stare into them until he floated away while Dusty's heart beat frantically against his skin and her tail thwopped against the sheet.

His mother had been gone more days then he knew how to count. And he didn't know where she had gone. But Dusty the dog lay against his side, occasionally sighing. Fred pulled the sheet off the bed and dragged it into the living room where his father was sitting on the couch. *Hernando's Hideaway, Olay!*

"Where's Mom?" he asked, sweating in his underwear and no shirt even as the dusty blades of an old metal fan spun lines of light across the brown carpet.

His father sat on the couch printed with daisies and sunflowers, his head bent over his knees, and stared at the ground. There was a blank sketchbook beside him covered with circles and lines. "What's this one we're listening to?" his father mumbled.

" 'Hernando's Hideaway.' "

"Who by?" His father didn't look up.

"Where's Mom?"

"I don't know." He said this as if it were a tape loop, as if he were a loop, and the days were like that too, loops of each other.

Fred heard Dusty thud onto the floor; he listened to the jingle of her tags. The jingle of a dog stretch. The jingle that meant he'd see her soon. The other morning he'd seen his mother in the kitchen doorway.

His dad's glasses—Buddy Holly glasses his mom called them—were foggy. He took them off and rubbed his squinty eyes. He rose from the couch and stared out the window, the thick frames dangling from his hand. Fred stared also. Heat like the tongue of a cartoon devil warped the dust, the scraggly trees, and the purple knapweed. He looked at his father, his eyes puffy, his face unshaven and slack, but his father was looking out the window. "You must know whose version," his father said absently.

He shook his head and sucked on his forefinger. It tasted like the ground. The TV was on. Silent cartoons turned the brown carpet bluish. The old lady in the shoe wagged her bony finger, and her many wild children, their black hair rising like hair on the backs of cats, whopped each other with pillows. *If you have so many children, and you don't know what to do, just take a little clue from the old lady in the shoe,* Fred whispered. Feathers floated past the old lady's face; her hair hung in cartoon clumps over her eyes. She reached behind her back and pulled out a jug and drank from it. Then the circle ate the screen—the wild children, the pillows, the drifting feathers, the inside of the shoe—until all that remained was the cameo of the old woman smiling and drinking, drinking and smiling, and then she too, just like everything else, disappeared.

"Is Mom at school?" Fred asked as the credits for the next cartoon began. Maybe she was in the library reading. Sometimes Fred and his father got to visit her in the library where she'd show Fred the stories she was reading, just like he read stories in school. Her stories were ghost stories and fairy tales and stories about Samurai and monkeys and bamboo gardens. There were even pictures in her books just like there were pictures in his books.

"I don't think so," his father said, statue-like by the window. Fred fell into the flowered couch, dragging the sheet with him, while a little boy swung his school books on the end of a string and whistled as he walked down the street. Crumbs on the couch itched his sticky legs. He held a corner of the sheet in his fist. He couldn't hear the boy's whistle, but he could see the boy's puffed cheeks—and he'd seen the cartoon more times than he could count. He'd seen it with his mother, and he'd seen it with his father and they'd all seen it together. Some days he'd helped his father make tapes of cartoons—*okay Freddy, which one next? You choose, then I choose*—while his mother was at school. Everyday she was at school. She rode her bike into school, down the long empty highway lined with sagebrush and knapweed and into town.

Once his father had taken him to the dollar store where he bought piles of dollar videos—*Cartoons R Fun*. From these they made tapes—one was all Max Fleischer, his father's favorite cartoonist. At the dollar store his father had let Fred buy one thing. Fred wanted a Power Ranger figure because that's what Tommy Norgen had brought to show and tell. "You don't really want that, do you Freddy?" his father said. "Why don't you look a little more." Fred found a pair of blue plastic sunglasses big like his mom's sunglasses. They made the whole world blue. He stared down at the Power Ranger in one hand and the glasses in another. He wore the glasses home in the truck. "Blue house, blue gas station, blue rock, blue truck, blue lady with a blue baby, blue grass, blue train."

The house smelled like old food. Fred fiddled with loose threads on the couch. He studied the sketchbook, but nothing looked like a cartoon, except for the smallest flower in one corner. It looked like a flower Fred could have drawn, a circle like a blank face, pedals like an inverted crown, and little waving leaves like arms.

On the TV, the spotted dog with the black patch over its eye pulled at the boy's pant leg, and the boy picked up the dog and laughed. "That dog is so damn cute," his mother used to say. "Yeah," Fred would giggle. Once she'd made his father draw a dog like that, a dog with a little patch over its eye. Fred had stared from the picture to his mother hugging his father's neck to the picture again. It looked just like that cute dog. He'd had it on his wall for a long time, but now it was gone, and he didn't know where. Gone too were the cartoons his father had drawn of his mother, one of her like Betty Boop only more stick-like standing with her hand on her hip, one of her drinking a beer on the flowered couch, her eyes sparkly blue cartoon stones, a dimple in her cheek like Olive Oyl's, red hair like a boy's, and knobby knees poking out of a small green paisley dress, a real dress she loved to wear. "Hernando's Hideaway" had ended and now "Blue Skies" played. Nothing played the same. The discs spun and shifted and sorted in the machine, and nothing was ever the same, except that there was always music and always the tape of Max Fleischer cartoons, at least it had been that way since his mother had been gone. He couldn't count how many days.

Dusty crawled up on the couch beside him, rested her nose in his lap, and sighed. *Blue skies, blue skies, shinin' on me, just shinin' on me.*

His father pulled the sketchbook out from under her tail. Dusty didn't move. He stood at his drawing table by the window and picked up a pencil.

"What're you drawing?"

He shrugged.

His father's hand moved in hard little x's across the page.

"Is mom coming home tonight?" he asked as he petted back Dusty's long ears, pulling damp hairs from the corners of her mouth.

His father turned to look at him, his eyes soft and shiny and unfamiliar, like the whole world had become unfamiliar. He opened his mouth, then looked away. "Daddy needs to work alone, Freddy," he said finally, as if his voice were half caught in his throat. Tonight his mom would not come home and his dad would not go to work at the bar, just like last night and the night before that. His father took the sketch pad and went upstairs.

Fred watched cartoon credits then stared at the white curving ceiling, like the inside of a plastic cave. Finally, he lifted Dusty's big head off his thigh, damp from her slobber, and got up. She trotted after him. He picked up a white T-shirt and big khaki shorts from the floor. The shorts drooped, and the shirt hung outside them. He'd been wearing them for as many days as he could count. He remembered wearing them with his mother when they went to the grocery store last, how she tucked his shirt in as they got out of the car. The shirt still had the stain from the ice cream sandwich she'd bought him that day. He pushed at the edges of the shirt, but some of it still hung out from the elastic in his shorts. He put on dirty white socks and his tennis shoes and tied the laces into knots because he'd forgotten how to do bows. Sometimes he could do it, but after awhile he needed to be reminded.

The kitchen stunk like rotten fruit. There was a stack of blue plates on a stack of phonebooks under the phone on the wall. In the garbage were paper plates soaked with red grease stains from sloppy joes. The plastic container his father got the sloppy joe meat out of sat on the counter unwashed. He was tired of sloppy joes. There was a piece of toast with a few bites out of it on the counter next to the glass coffee pitcher half-filled with coffee. He ate most of the rest of it standing in the kitchen then wiped his hands on his shirt and drank some water from a half-filled glass. His stomach felt tight from wanting to eat and tight also from eating.

His blue plastic shades were on the very edge of the counter. He pulled open the broom closet door—his mother had been standing here this morning, or was that yesterday morning? Was she still here? A dustpan clattered out, a mop fell across the cracked linoleum, and Dusty skittered across the floor. There was no mother. Maybe she was outside.

The plastic shades rested on the tip of his nose and reached as far as his hairline. The tips of them poked out past the backs of his ears. He fake smiled, and his cheeks pressed against the plastic. He unsmiled, smiled again, unsmiled. They didn't fall off. The world was blue. He stepped into the bathroom and looked into the medicine cabinet mirror. The glasses took up most of his face. His mother wore glasses that were big on her face too. His eyes looked back at him through the plastic like fly eyes. Sometimes if he looked closely, he could see his mother's eyes through the gray of her sunglasses, but he could never see his father's eyes through his sunglasses. He'd only see himself little, with a big head and a tiny body like a bug mirrored back at him.

Maybe his blue plastic glasses were secret glasses that would let him see things other people couldn't see, like his mother. Maybe she'd been there all along, and that's why he saw her the other morning—maybe he'd been wearing his blue plastic shades. He couldn't remember. She was standing in the kitchen. He took off the glasses, and she was gone. He put the glasses back on, and she was still gone. Dusty sat down on his foot and leaned against his leg. Fred stared into the darkened kitchen, at the closet door where she'd just stood. Dusty pressed her nose against his loose hand. Fred put the glasses back on. No mother.

"Let's go, Dusty," he said, because that's what his mom says, *Let's go*, and Dusty thumped her tail against the linoleum.

Outside was hotter than inside, summer hot, out-of-kindergarten hot, hot. Usually his mother or father was with him when he was outside. They walked on the weekend days when she didn't have to go to school. The world felt big without a grownup next to him.

Freddy.

He squinted up at the upstairs porch, the porch that was only attached to his parents' room. He wasn't allowed to walk up the wooden stairs on the outside because the stairs shook and creaked. For a moment she was there in a night dress, waving at him, an all-blue mother, and then she wasn't there. He stared until blue spots jumped about his eyes, and sweat formed under the plastic glasses. He shaded his face with his hand, but she was still gone.

He walked behind the house, behind the metal dome like an upside down U his mom said you could park a small airplane in. *Why you'd want to*, she'd said, *beats me*. Other houses didn't look like this house. Cheney had lots of houses, but none of them had a metal dome. From the outside, it looked like a cartoon house.

In the front was a regular house with two stories and a porch, but from the side, you could see the dome.

He walked through cheat grass that clung to his ankles. Mourning doves cooed. "Owls," he'd said once to his mother, stopping in the field so he could hear them over the shuffle of their feet in the dry grass. "Mourning doves," she said. "Owls hoot at night, and mourning doves coo in the morning." "Coo?" "Coo coo," she said. "Coo coo," he cooed. "Coo," and she bent down and cooed into his neck until he giggled so much he'd lost his balance and had fallen over. He wanted to throw his body into hers right now, slam against her so she could feel him, grab her legs so she couldn't get away. The coos sounded ghostly and sad.

In front of him, sage and knapweed and thistle stretched in all directions, and far off was a cluster of scrubby pines. The knapweed flowers didn't look purple. They looked blue. And the fist-sized prickly thistle flowers, once alternately white or purple, were all blue. And the white fuzzy plants his mom called little sunflowers didn't look white. Their yellow flowers were dried up and gone now. The leaves looked like pairs of blue dancing slippers. Beyond the pine grove were the beginnings of hills blue in the bright summer morning. He set off through the brush blowing air through his mouth trying to whistle, but there was no whistle, only the empty shuffle of tunes in his head. Dusty bounded away and back, away and back, and Fred ran his palms across the tops of plants. Sometimes he and his mom walked back here, and sometimes all four of them walked. His mom pointed things out, like this is where Little Mouse peeps out to see the day, and if the day looks sour, Little Mouse jumps back in her hole and sleeps.

Fred stared at the ground looking for mouse holes. The dirt swelled into clumps, so he bent down and stared at them, around them, through the legs of knapweed and at the tiny knapweed flowers, now like the blue stars in his father's cartoon about the dreamers where the moon is an old drunk throwing bottles at the horizon to keep the sun down. A spider scuttled out from under a stone, and Fred crept back a step. It scratched at the dirt with its many legs, like a crab on the surface of a star.

Maybe there was somewhere he needed to be. Maybe if he walked as far as the trees he would find his mother, like in the book: *are you my mother? the little bird asked.* How many nights ago had she read that? They had it in the kindergarten too, and he'd memorized it and read it to Tommy Norgen and Brittany Teel. Sweat had formed behind his knees from bending. He tore the purple-blue flowers off the knapweed. His fingers prickled and burned. He tossed the flowers around him like a ritual, like his mother burning sage in the house to keep out the ghosts.

He heard the crying then like he'd heard the crying before. It seemed to be all around him, but when he looked back at the house, the dome was little, and he couldn't decide where the crying came from. Choking and sniffing and crying. He looked up into the sky; blue rings circled the sun, and he felt dizzy and faint and wondered if he were sleeping, the wailing surrounding him. He'd never been out this far into the field by himself. He heard Dusty's tags jingling closer and closer still and turned and watched her gallop as if in slow motion toward him, her ears flopping up and down, her long long tongue wagging out of her smiling mouth.

He kept walking, Dusty panting by his side, the sun beating down on his bare arms and knees, everything blue. The crying fell away from him, dissipated into the blue air so that only its echoes rang in his inner ear. He stopped and cocked his head straining to hear, but there was no discerning it, discerning the inside from the outside. His head buzzed with heat and echoes and the small sounds of bugs.

He kept walking, the scrub pines his mother called Piney Grove growing larger, as if they were lurching toward him and not the other way around. There was a circle of trees where they'd had sandwiches she called The Schoolhouse, and there was an old refrigerator dumped on its side without a door. He'd seen a deer with his mother in Piney Grove. She'd grabbed Dusty's collar, and they'd watched the deer in parts through the trees bending its thick neck and scratching at the dirt with its nose. But then Dusty shook her head in protest, and at the jingle of her tags, the deer leapt away, bounded through the trees as if the trees weren't there at all. "How does she jump without knowing what's in front of her?" Fred asked.

"No one knows what's in front of them, Freddy," she'd said.

The trees ahead of him threw shadows across the desert. Dusty lay in the shade panting. Fred sat next to her, stretching his bare legs across the prickly ground. She rested her nose on the ground and sighed; her body heaved slowly under his hand on the back of her neck. The air hummed with crickets and the far away sound of an occasional car on the highway in front of their house. Dusty lifted her head and resumed her panting. It rattled in the still air like the rattling of the air conditioner nailed into the window in the house. "Let's go, Dusty," he said after awhile.

On the edge of Piney Grove was a fence, and beyond that, the brown desert brush rose and fell in small mounds. He'd never been beyond the fence. His mother always made sure he and Dusty stayed away from it because it was barbed wire, *like at a jail*, she'd said once. But today his mother wasn't there, and he didn't know where she was, and it seemed to him that beyond that fence might be the place she was, out of jail. The fence was rusty and punctuated by small stars of metal. The posts were made of sticks, like the staff the old man of the woods carries. According to his mother, the old man of the woods slept in the depressions in Piney Grove and around tree roots. He wore a crumpled, black paper hat and tapped the earth with a staff when he walked. He was dusty and wore gray and brown and pale green and was hard to see because he blended into the desert.

"Why does the old man of the woods wear a paper hat?" he'd asked his mother on one of their picnics.

She looked off toward the fence as if she were thinking. "Because he's a ghost."

"Is he a good ghost or a bad ghost?"

"The old man of the woods is neither a good ghost nor a bad ghost."

He looked at her, ready to ask more, but she was thinking, and so he waited. "The people who loved him when he was alive burned the paper hat for him so he'd have something to protect his head in the afterlife."

Dusty crawled under the fence, her back rubbing against one of the stars, and sniffed the ground of the world beyond. There was an orange sign that said "No Trespassing" and "No Hunting." His mother had read him the sign. Fred crawled under the fence, but his shirt got caught on a star and the star scratched his back. He reached to unhook it, and another star stuck into the skin on his arm. He ripped his arm away and cried out. He lay on his stomach, his shirt tented above him hooked to the wire star. A thick drop of blood oozed from the cut on his arm. He crawled forward pulling the wire with him until finally he heard the short rip of the shirt, and it sprung loose. As he tried to stand, the barb ran along his bare lower back, and he broke into tears. Free of the wire, he sat in the dirt sucking the blood on his arm and cry-ing. He looked back at the house, but the house was gone. There was only the maze of trees and glimpses of the familiar knapweed field beyond. He was hungry and hot. Tears dropped off his cheek and ran down his neck. Dusty lay down beside him panting, her slobber dampening his splotchy red legs.

Tears fogged the blue plastic shades. He pulled them off; the brightness stung. His crying grew to a choking bawl, his chin quivering. "Mommy," he cried, but no one came. "Daddy," but no one came. The silence answered, crickets and the buzzing of tiny bugs and the ringing of the heat. He hiccupped and choked and hid his face in his hands. His arm hurt and his back hurt, and he felt ashamed for his ripped shirt. He was hungry, and he'd never known no one to be there for him. He rolled on his side and hung onto Dusty crying into her soft spotted coat. She tensed and tried to wiggle away, but he held tight until finally she licked frantically at his face. He waited. Because someone would come. He couldn't imagine no one coming. Always someone had come—when he tried to stand on the slide and fell, Ms. Pat had been there. When he was running down the sidewalk in Cheney and fell on his face, scraping his wrists on the cement so that white flakes of skin tore loose and dots of blood sprung up, his mother had been there, and he'd clung to her neck and bawled into her shirt. His father had been there in the night when a ghost had chased him through an empty house and into a shallow grave. He'd woken up screaming, and his father was there, as if he'd heard Fred even before the scream had started, there switching on the light, telling him a new story about the rain babies, *the rain babies are born in the spring*, pushing the hair off his forehead, until he'd felt himself sleepy and disappeared.

He wanted to disappear now, feel himself sleepy, drift away, like he drifted away in the theatre when his parents took him to see his first movie. The darkness descended, and the chair was floaty, and the flicker of the screen was a life on the other side of a window. Where was his mother? He wiped his face with his bare arm, wiped at the blood with the front of his shirt and got up. The glasses dangled from his hand. He wiped the sweaty lenses clean on his shirt just like his father had wiped his Buddy Holly glasses on his shirt that morning. "Why are they Buddy Holly's glasses?" he'd asked his mom. "Buddy Holly was an old time rock singer, and he died in a plane crash. He had glasses just like your dad's." At home she'd played him a Buddy Holly record and they'd jumped around the living room together, waving their hands in the air like they were dancing. Fred liked to watch the needle running in the records' groves. His friends didn't have records.

"Let's go, Dusty," he said and put the glasses back on. The world was blue again, and the pain from his cuts turned into a dull ache that soon disappeared as he walked. Dusty's tags jingled in the silence as she trotted beside him. She'd given up roaming in large circles and chasing bugs and birds and mice hidden in the brush. She hung her head lower than her body and walked with the same steady determination that kept Fred going. As they walked gradually up a swell of earth, the prickly grass and knapweed and thistle gave way to more and more sage and scattered rocks.

On the high ground, Fred could see further than he'd ever been able to see in the desert, maybe further than he'd ever seen anywhere. There was layer upon layer of tiny ridges, purple and brown and dull green, bluish in the distance. There were grassy indents, and clusters of trees that rose up out of holes in the earth. There were deep depressions and rocky plateaus like in Roadrunner cartoons. He stumbled upon a little trail he thought was a deer trail. In the winter, he and his mom and his dad would follow deer trails behind the house, all three in their orange hats so they wouldn't get shot by the hunters, even though they never saw hunters and never saw their tracks, though often they'd hear the far-off pop of a gun. Here the trail was dusty, but Fred could see the faint tracks of deer. The deer trails were like the trails behind the playground older kids used on their way home from school. The little kids like him ran back and forth along the trails during recess.

He followed the deer trail, Dusty dropping in line behind him. They walked above a deep depression where trees sprang up along the edge of a small lake. The shore was cracked dry mud, and a swell of tiny bugs hovered over the surface of the diminishing water. The trail wound down alongside the tiny lake and through an opening between two rock formations. From above, Fred could see a stretch of desert and then an expanse of trees much bigger than Piney Grove. He stood on a rocky outcropping and looked across the desert, following the deer trail with his eyes. Dusty suddenly leaped in front of him and ran off, her legs kicking out behind her fat body as if her body should give away, but it didn't. Far away, a coyote loped across the desert. Fred stood stiff and still.

"Are coyotes evil?"

"There's no such thing as evil, Freddy," his mother had said.

Still, he felt a shock of fear. "Dusty!" he hollered, but his tiny voice dissipated into the open space, and Dusty kept running until she disappeared into the far away trees. He clambered down the rocks, but his shoelace got caught under his foot, his foot turned on its side, and he fell forward, scraping his knee badly on a jagged rock. He sat down under a tree and examined the cut. It was longer than his hand, and it hurt. Maybe he could have seen his house when he was on the ridge, but now that he'd climbed down, he couldn't see anything but the desert ahead and the dark cluster of far-off trees. He stared through his blue glasses into the wound, but could see nothing but a foggy mess. He pulled off the glasses. His leg looked yellow in the sharp new light. A large hunk of skin had been peeled back, and he could see the inside of his leg, a white and red complex of muscle and tissue. Besides the new gash, both legs were covered with tiny scratches and spotted red from a sunburn just beginning to show itself. A thin stream of blood cascaded down the back of his calf. He twisted his leg around and followed it to the top of his white socks now spotted with blood. He imagined his shoe filling up with blood. His one lace had come untied. He tied it into a knot and tucked the ends under the crisscrossing lace. Without the glasses, he could see the bright moss like paint on the rocks, yellow and rusty red and green. "Dusty," he called again, only this time not so loud. He felt like Wile E. Coyote flattened by a boulder.

For a moment he watched the sky. Thick clouds in the distance seemed to be rolling toward him. Then he wiped the shades off on his T-shirt, put them back on, and got up. He walked out into the desert, the heat bearing down on him, the world muted blue. His leg ached, and he walked slower, favoring the other. He wished he had a staff like the old man of the woods. Maybe in the big trees he'd find a staff. At least the big trees would be shady. And maybe he'd find Dusty. He had to find Dusty. He walked past mullein plants, three of them, one twice his height with wide fuzzy leaves as long as his arm and stalks in the center clustered with hundreds of pea-sized buds; only the tips above his head were yellow with bloom like the tips of long thin candles or giant flashlights. Last Halloween, his mother had soaked dried mullein stalks in oil, and they'd lit them outside and watched them pop like firecrackers.

"Dusty!" he called occasionally with little conviction as he stumbled through the prickly brush. A breeze rustled the dried grasses as the blue clouds humped closer. He followed a deer trail through the wide expanse of sage and knapweed. A small panic brewed in his chest, but he pressed it down and kept going, calling and tripping over loose rock and clumps of vetch. He felt a pang of hunger. Had they eaten sloppy joes last night? Was he sick last night? Hadn't his mother visited him?

Up ahead the land looked different again. It looked like the trees were lining an enormous valley, and as he got closer, he could see cliffs on the opposite side of the valley, rows of cliffs, cliffs on top of cliffs, and as he got closer still he saw that the valley was a long narrow canyon lake, a shocking expanse of blue surrounded by enormous cliffs. When he saw it he stopped suddenly. Light sparked off the blue water, millions of pinpoints of sunlight. Even the sky seemed to take on the color of the water. It was difficult to tell just how far away it was because it was so big. It gave him a sense of vertigo that only increased the closer he got. He understood now that this is why he'd seen all the trees. They were growing around the lake and across the lake.

Fred stood near the edge of the cliff. Off to the left, there were more cliffs, big cliffs, only they were very far below him. There were layers of cliffs and giant rock outcroppings that jutted into the lake. The still lake reflected the cliffs so that at moments it was unclear what were real cliffs and what were not. He felt dizzy and hazy and awestruck. The burst of blue floating in the blue lenses of his glasses. He removed the glasses again and was flooded with the brilliant light of day. If he could not feel his feet on the ground, he would feel himself falling, and so he felt his feet on the ground, his eyes wide with light, light that poured through him as if the heat and the hunger had made his body soft and permeable. It was then he heard Dusty's tags. She loped toward him carrying something in her mouth and wagging her tail.

"Dusty!" The thing she was carrying was a sawed-off deer leg. Without his glasses, he could see clearly the clean cut of the saw, the red inside of the deer leg, the corded muscles and stiffened flesh. "Drop it drop it drop it!" he yelled like his dad had yelled when Dusty once caught a marmot. "Drop it!"

Dusty was a good dog. She dropped it and ran to him, her head low, her body wagging. Fred looked back at the lake only briefly, but in that moment he understood something. His mother was not coming back.

He held Dusty's collar and together they turned away from the lake. He didn't know if he'd been sick last night, but he no longer wondered. He felt sick right now, and that seemed to be the only thing that mattered. His ankles felt itchy and prickly where cheat grass clung to the inside of his socks. He shoved the sunglasses in his pocket and stared at the ground to keep from tripping. He watched his feet: the ends of his shoelaces had come out of their holding place under the rest of the lace and flopped on either side of his shoes.

The sun had crossed the center of the sky, and as they walked, the desert light grew muted and soft. The puffy clouds had thinned and spread across the sky like gauze, occasionally masking the brightness and heat of the sun. He watched the shadows of clouds darken the plants. A small breeze dried the sweat on the back of his neck and behind his knees. The smell of sage rose from the desert dirt, and clusters of small white flowers quivered. Light-headed with hunger, his skin burning despite the cooling air, he concentrated hard on the deer paths making his way back the way he'd come as best he could.

⸻

By the time Fred was in clear sight of his house, the thin veil of clouds had turned half pink. He watched his father running as if in slow motion through the purple knapweed. He felt dazed and stunned, jolted out of the giant world he'd navigated through all day. His father looked like a crazy cartoon character, his face contorted and twisted, breathing so loud that even from far away Fred could feel the pressure of his father's heart and blood surrounding him.

"Freddy, Jesus, Freddy," he said, out of breath, and grabbed Fred and picked him off the ground and hugged him close to his sweaty body. "Jesus Freddy, where have you been? Jesus, I'm sorry. I'm so sorry. I'm so sorry." Fred felt his father's tears on his cheek and neck like he'd felt his mother's cooing in his neck. Finally, he put Fred down, held his arms, and, crouching on the ground in front of him, looked into his face.

"I'm so sorry, Freddy," he said again, his glasses foggy white. "I'm so sorry." He wiped the hair off Fred's forehead. "Are you okay?"

Fred pointed at the gash on his leg, now hard with dried, rusty blood. His father held his knee, and Fred leaned against his shoulder for balance.

"Does it hurt?"

"Mm hmm."

"Okay, kiddo," his father said and picked Fred off the ground and carried him through the purple knapweed. The last time he remembered being carried was when he'd fallen asleep in the car after his mother took him to visit his father at the bar where he worked, and they'd sat outside and had drinks on the patio. He'd had a kiddy cocktail with a paper umbrella and two cherries. He'd woken up draped in his mother's arms, his cheek against her shoulder, and looked up into her face; she had a small, crooked smile. Right now he wished he'd never closed his eyes, pretending to be asleep. Now, he looked over his father's shoulder at the diminishing desert as if he were leaving part of himself behind.

Inside Fred sat on the counter while his father dabbed at the wound on his leg with a gauze pad. It hurt, but Fred didn't flinch. His father applied a cool clear worm of Neosporin, covered the wound with another gauze pad, and wrapped an Ace bandage around his calf. He washed Fred's face with a washcloth and rubbed aloe all over his arms and legs. Neither spoke. He found two ticks around Fred's ankles and one more in his head. Dusty lay with her nose on the kitchen floor watching them. No music was playing, and the TV was turned off. His father made them French toast, and Fred drank glass after glass of water. Then Fred sat at the kitchen table and watched his father clean the dishes and sweep the floor. He felt comforted by the kitchen's yellow light and the close walls.

It was winter and Fred stood at the edge of the lake, now covered with snow, an enormous expanse of white. He felt the same vertigo; he could hear the snow falling around him, big flakes of it rubbing up against one another, shuffle, shuffle, shuffle. The old man of the woods in his crumpled black paper hat approached him. He was carrying a sawed-off deer leg. Fred tried to scream, but nothing would come out. And then he was lying in the darkness, the muted square of porch light through his window shade just becoming decipherable. He held back the scream. He got up and switched on the light. He lay back down in bed and began to whisper to himself. *The man of the woods is neither good nor bad. There is no such thing as evil, Freddy. Rain babies are born in the spring.* Then he patted himself on the forehead.

His body stung from sunburn. He stared at the ceiling and still could not sleep. He got out of bed again, padded into the kitchen, and poured himself a glass of water. He went into the living room and turned on the TV. Dusty climbed quietly up beside him. The Max Fleischer tape began in the middle of *The Cobweb Hotel.* In it, two newlywed flies go to a spider's hotel only to find themselves in a trap. The beds are actually webs spun by the spider. Fred watched as the lady fly squeaked helplessly, her arms and legs pinned to the spider's web while the man fly cut at the web with a giant razor blade.

"Freddy?" His father stood at the bottom of the stairs in a white T-shirt and his striped boxers. Fred hadn't even heard him come down. "Are you alright?"

"Uh huh," Fred said without looking away from the TV.

His father sat down beside him, put his head in his palms, and wept. It was the weeping Fred had been hearing since his mother had been gone. He touched his father's head briefly. The air from the fan skittering across his sunburned legs made him chilly. He pulled the sheet he'd left from the morning over them and held onto the corner.

"Daddy," he said.

"Yeah Fred."

"Can we burn a paper hat for mom?"

He looked at Fred with his glasses off, his eyes squinty. "Sure we can," he said.

"Have some water." Fred handed him the glass.

His father drank down the water, and then they sat in silence and watched as the two flies and their luggage flew away.

The Grandmother's Vision

The grandmother, Carolina, had gathered all the family members who were still alive and not incarcerated to the lake to scatter her youngest son's ashes. One-armed Billy, Charlotte, and Duke with his metal canes were the only three of the seven who fit the bill, except for Jordan, who even Carolina knew better than to ever allow on the family property again—if he wasn't currently incarcerated, no doubt he should be. A half-dozen or more grandchildren, most of whom she couldn't identify, played around the campfire in true Stevenson fashion: inventive in their insults, *smells like a cat crawled up your butthole and died*; sulking around hitting things, including each other, with sticks; crawling into cars and trucks and onto motorcycles trying to start them with paperclips and coat hangers as if by some magic beyond their understanding, anything to hear a motor, to be in control of all that noise and speed. What was there to keep track of? They were all the same as the generation before, lanky anxious boys and slutty pimply girls who would turn into overweight, angry women.

It hadn't been an hour since the scattering of Ben's ashes from the dock (where one kid knocked a little girl into the water—she rose screaming to the surface, not only because she couldn't swim but because she was covered in her uncle's ashy bones—*it's all OVER me!*), and already they were lighting things on fire and throwing rocks. The prayer circle, where everyone had held hands and bent their heads to the ground, had no effect.

"You leave that dog alone!" Carolina shouted as an anonymous child came at Ben's dog with a stick, the dog unwittingly smiling, and then, seeing the swing of the stick, tucking her tail between her legs, crouching low, as if to receive her punishment.

The only one of them she cared a crap for was Mickey, Jordan's only son, whose thin face looked out the trailer window, his hearing aid curled around his ear like a security blanket. He'd stayed in there all weekend, would have nothing to do with any of them, despite the fact that she was paying his bills. She'd let him move into Ben's trailer after Ben had moved in with her to die. Billy and Duke told her not to, that she was enabling his habit, said her "soft spot" for him was ruining her better judgment—the same soft spot that had allowed Ben to live in the trailer rent-free and drink himself to death. But she knew better. Because she could hear inside their heads. It was this ability to hear what was not spoken that had compelled her, at age 80, to drive 24 hours, through two states, and pick up Ben after he broke his collar bone diving into cement (the dock he jumped off of didn't hang over the water). When she arrived, she'd found the stiff body of his pit bull, poisoned, he claimed, by Jordan (she could not deny this likelihood), the trailer with no electricity, small fish carcasses, terrible tasteless meals from the lake, littering the porch. It was the hearing that had driven her back a few years later to take Ben and his new dog, a smiling, lanky mutt he'd named Carolina, to Oregon again where he'd lived with her until his liver shut down six months later, leaving Carolina with the bouncy, tail wagging tri-colored dog of her namesake.

The air smelled of campfire, bacon and pancakes, and lake. The fire had been going since last night, but the cooking was all done on fancy cookstoves the women had set up on a white plastic table under an awning of the RV. It had rained the entire first day the family had gathered, which might explain why no one let the fire die out once they were able to get it going good and why their camp looked like a tent city of blue tarps. Fat Charlotte and Duke's wife (Carolina had forgotten her name—but what did it matter—she was just like all the rest—overstuffed, over-painted, oversexed and wasteful) sat in fancy fold-up chairs under the awning drinking coffee dosed with their fancy Bailey's flavored creamer packs. But who was she to judge them for all their gear, she who enjoyed the comfort of the RV at night? Still, she heard nothing from them but dead air. From all of them, the aggressive men and the slutty women, she'd heard nothing but a vacuous buzzing.

The only child of hers whose thoughts she'd been able to hear had been Ben. It was not a sense of knowing what he felt so much as a recording of the noise inside his head, the repetitive humming of the choruses of songs—"Pop Goes the Weasel" and "John Jacob Jingle Heimer Schmidt" and rock songs with lyrics she hadn't recognized. She'd heard the stories he told himself, even when he never spoke them. They'd come to her cold nights when the snowy stillness outside had made her feel trapped: a hummingbird kept a skinny bear alive by feeding him water a beakful at a time. The bear unzipped his fur and the skeleton boy emerged. She, too, had been kept alive by drops once, drops from a hospital tube snaking into her arm. What was it she'd done to deserve that particular beating? Tried to pull the needle out of her oldest son's arm that his father had put there? It's hard to remember. Objecting hadn't changed anything.

The professor next door with his pretentious English cap was watching the Stevenson family reunion from his porch, his new agey whore of a wife with all the scarves standing beside him. She was tired of these goddamn neighbors and their complaints, which came in the form of Billy whining on the other end of the phone line to her. "What do you want me to do about it?" she'd say. Didn't matter whether it was Ben or Mickey living in the trailer, they were full of complaints. Where else, she wanted to ask, did these neighbors think these boys could live if not under the protection of their family? They'd be so lucky—she guessed that stupid professor smoked a pipe—to have a grandmother as generous as her. Rich stingy bastards, his parents, that's what she guessed, by the looks of him. It was like they were watching a circus, and elephants were crapping in their backyard. Let them watch. She owned most of the land around here, three lots worth. And not one of her grandchildren had so much as spit on anyone else's property.

Mickey has guests at the trailer, a skinny woman and a skinny man and a small boy. The boy has disappeared among the grandchildren. She can't tell which one he is. At night the boy sleeps in the car; the night it rained, the parents put a blanket over the broken window. She does not speculate why any of this is happening, why Mickey hasn't come out of the house or why the child sleeps in the car, or why the family is there at all. She has not listened to Billy, even as he has spoken to her of the problem. She does not care about what the problem may be. It is the same as all the other problems, and she's had enough of them. And it doesn't change how she feels about Mickey, who is the exact image of her boy Ben. With the exact same squeaky voice and the same shy manner. The same confusion and guardedness in his eyes. She remembers him the day she met him. His father is about to go to jail for raping a girl with Down's Syndrome. Mickey is seven, looking at the ground; in his head she hears classical music. At first she does not realize this sound is coming from this child, but then it is as clear as a new radio with stereophonic speakers. She will never forgot this sound, how it filled her up entirely, how for a moment she thought she might cry out at the pain of it, the sorrow in all that beautiful noise. She could not hug Jordan that day when his soon-to-be-ex-wife drove him away to prison. But she put her old hands on Mickey's shoulders and felt the vibration of the music move through the both of them.

Carolina sits on a lawn chair near the awning where the women are cooking, but in the sun because after all the rain, it feels good to have the sun on her skin. A mist hangs over the lake, though it could be the campfire smoke. Three faces now peer out through the parted curtains, which are really just blankets and sheets, of the trailer window.

"Godammit," Billy says. "I'm tired of this shit," and strides up to the trailer, his one armless sleeve swinging, his baseball hat pulled down low on his forehead, and his reddish hair falling down his back like a girl's.

There's that one, Carolina thinks, but even as she thinks it she can't remember a damn thing about Billy, or how he lost the arm. She hears the beating of his fist on the door.

"Leave it alone," the other brother says after a while. "You just gonna make it worse."

"You little fucker!" Billy yells and steps away from the door.

Just when his back is turned, the door flies open and Mickey comes out swinging a baseball bat, just missing Billy's head. Billy spins around, his hair whipping across his cheek. "Shit," he says as he backs toward the campfire.

Mickey stands at the top of the porch's three crooked steps. His pants hang at his waist, below the line of his underwear. They hang halfway down his butt. His face is scabby and yellow; the hearing aid clings to his ear like a worm.

The grandmother watches Mickey's mouth moving but cannot comprehend the words. She hears his high, frantic voice as if it is the fire hissing and screaming at them all. His contorted expression reminds her of a carnival freak she saw once as a child, a man who could stick a long needle in one cheek and out the other. The skinny mother of the child who sleeps in the car is dancing around the porch like it's on fire, like she's barefoot and can't avoid the flames, even though she keeps trying.

The grandmother watches with the same bewilderment she'd watched the night the teenage Jordan had taken the young girl down to the pond, unwitting Ben following behind, sucking nervously on his fingers. She'd heard the cry, and she'd heard about the missing child days later.

She hears the faintest crackling of classical music, as if she'd tuned into a radio station in a snow storm. "We're asking for your help, friends," a man interrupts. "Just once a year. Call in now to keep the music alive." And then the crackling again.

"Fuck you all! Get the fucking hell outa here—I'm sicka all you fuckers—take that old bitch and that damn dog with you!" Carolina, as if aware he's talking about her, raises her white and black head from the ground, her eyebrows comically arched triangles of brown. She cocks her head back and forth, her enormous ears like radar.

The grandmother rises from her lawn chair. She walks toward the porch. The dog springs up from the ground and runs to her, wagging her black-tipped tail. She presses her body against the grandmother's knees. Someone from the depths of the trailer puts a blanket around Mickey's shoulders, as if to somehow stop his mad shaking. Perhaps, she thinks now, she should have said something about the girl Jordan dumped in the pond. But even this thought is on a frequency in need of too much support to survive. The dog pushes her nose into the grandmother's hand. The boy on the porch wears a coat of crows.

The Island of Cats

The surface of the water is the color of metal. Gray reflects gray. The canoe slips into steely water. Mud squelches under Billy's tennis shoes like weight sucking him into the shoreline. This weight feels right, normal, the slow sucking of each step, the slow and constant effort. He cannot imagine living without the weight. The weight is who he is. This boat trip is who he is. He would rather die than be anything other than who he is. He feels the weight of waking on his eyelids, and that feels right in the gray, predawn morning. The sand is pocked with small holes dug by fiddler crabs. Tiny mounds of excess mud throw hive-like shadows across the shore cut by the wavy shadows of mangrove roots. Everything will go on living. The roots will thrust themselves, with the slow weight of life, out of the mud and sand will collect around them with each wave, little as they are here on an inland curve of the Intracoastal Waterway. The stern of the canoe between his knees, he wades into the murky water. It seeps in through the cotton of his tennis shoes and hugs his feet. He stares at his pale knees poking out from tan pants ripped into shorts, his dirty tennis shoes distorted under the six inches or so of water. He studies the line between the clear, sharp edges of his calf and the permeable image of his ankle and foot.

He will study this line, this distinction, all day in the horizon and imagine it into nonexistence. Mourning doves coo from the shore like tiny owls blurring the line between night and day.

He follows the edge of the boat to the center and climbs in, keeping his weight low. His bare knees against the metal bottom, he pulls out a red paddle and stabs at the mud with the handle and propels the boat forward. The mud kicks up like dust in slow motion. He moves to the stern of the canoe and paddles out, one stroke to the left, one to the right. One to the left, one to the right. Listening to the timed patterns of wood against water, the paddle distorted under the surface. The tips of his fingers are flattened and soft, the backs of his hands smooth, pale, hairless as if 33 years and countless jobs had left no mark—dishwasher, clerk, bellman, laundry worker.

Ahead, low mangrove islands litter the Intracostal Waterway. He paddles toward the closest of these. A blue heron stalks the shallows bending its head occasionally to the water. Egrets appear deeper in the mangroves, little flashes of white coming into fullness the closer he gets. And closer still, hundreds of fiddler crabs scuttle across the low tide shore, clambering on top of one another as the tide pulls in. He cannot distinguish them. All he sees is movement and a collective blur of purple—each crab's single giant claw, as big as their half-inch bodies. It is as if the sand itself is moving. Even from this far off he can hear the shuffle, the purple claws clicking, the frantic scurrying; it is the tiny sound of the world from which he's always hidden, the scuttling busyness of it, the lights and billboards and people in restaurants and stores. Here the sound is swallowed in the quiet morning, like a handful of lights, say lights of boats on the water, are swallowed by expanses of dark. In his world, it always seems to be the other way around: the lights of St. Petersburg swallow the darkness of the wild. The noise of people swallows his silence. The thousands of pieces of things swallow wholeness.

As he gets closer to the island, tails and paws and heads of cats weave in and out of mangrove roots. He rests the paddle over both knees and watches. A fat yellow cat rubbing against a tree startles and runs, a black and white cat leaps over a mangrove root and disappears. Water rubs against the canoe and the tip of the boat slips in between mangrove branches. Large broken whelk shells, bleached white and gray, litter the thin strip of sand. Hermit crabs shuffle into their holes among the pencil-sized mangrove sprouts. Cats dig their claws into sand and launch themselves into the brush. He wades through the water and ties the painter to a mangrove. He carries a small paper sack with a tuna fish sandwich he made last night. The stern of the canoe weaves slowly back and forth in the water, pulling at the pliable mangrove limb. He bends under mangroves where cats have left circles of whitish sand where they've slept. Tails flicker in the lattice of branches. Black tails and yellow tails flicking. He knows they are in the trees watching him, but as much as he looks, he cannot seem them.

He sits in the sand, digs his feet into the coolness left over from evening. He pulls out the sandwich. It is wrapped in wax paper. He bites into one half. The brown bread, two loaves for one dollar at Mr. C's discount grocery on Central Ave, is surprisingly soft. He wonders if this is his imagination, his way of making the meal more than it is, as if everything today will be more than anything ever was any other day of his life. It may be the best half a tuna fish sandwich he's ever had. He pulls the other half apart, lays out the wax paper, and scrapes the tuna fish onto it. He sucks on the soft bread until it's gone.

He follows a path through the mangroves, not a real path, but a path he can see, a path for a child or a small, bent man, one that only exists in the moment you're on it and never again. It is the type of path that reveals itself as you walk. There is no indecision on such a path. There could be nothing more right than your next step. And to a man who has never felt any step was ever right, who has worried himself into immobility, this path feels like the birth of a new world. It feels like a birthday party where there are actually loved ones and he actually loves them and he is the center of attention. It feels like a lottery he has won. It feels like a dream, so much so that he has to take stock of the things around him to make sure he is awake. He didn't know it would feel this way. If he'd known, he might have done this sooner.

Bits of sunlight strike his face. He moves in and out of sunlight as if the light were a pattern he memorized long ago. The type of sunlight you should see against your curtains as a child, when you lie in bed, each day the world fresh and new, and listen to the mourning doves cooing in the orange trees. Except for Billy, every morning the world has felt old and the sunlight stale, and the mourning doves only an echo of something in the background calling him away. All his life the doves have reminded him of something not yet happened. They have been thin ghosts calling. To his left triangles of gray water appear like puzzle pieces between branches, and to his right the mangroves give way to palmetto bushes, their wide palm-like fronds low to the ground.

Ahead the island curves inward. The tips of Australian pines rise above palmetto brush. Through the trees, silver glints like Morse code. It is the flashing of sunlight against the Hermit's giant mound of TV dinner trays, though Billy can only see glimpses of the pile through branches, until the spaces between waxy leaves grow larger and the mangroves open to a blue-brown plate of shallow water, and the sun splinters into hundreds of tin eyes, flickers of silver everywhere, like a disco dance ball moving across his face. Predawn has given way to a blinding early morning glare. The sand is wet again, and he is walking across a thin layer of clear water. Clouds of fine sand produced from his feet striking the bottom dissipate so quickly that the water is completely clear and undisturbed outside of the three-inch circle around each foot.

He knows the Hermit will be there, among the heaps of TV dinner trays and garbage, but now, all he can see is the magnificent heap, from this distance a pile of shine, a lost man's treasure, Jesus' one fish turned to millions of silver bellies. He's seen the Hermit twice, but each time he was too far away to see anything more than the small man's bent back retreating to higher ground among the pines. And those times he'd seen everything from the water only, days when he'd canoe slowly along the Intracoastal reaching with each stroke for a resonance, feeling the canoe's attempts at harmony with the motion of water, but always the thunking of his paddle strokes kept all parts dissonant.

He wades into the open lagoon, and the sand turns to muck that sucks and grabs at his tennis shoes. The water is up to his knees, and he can't see below his ankles. It smells gassy and acrid. The water is brown, though the surface of the lagoon as a whole appears blue. He feels the humps of clams deep under the sand and the occasional poke of a mangrove root still buried. Clusters of sea grass brush against his ankles. The sun shines like an enormous spotlight on the grandiose heap of TV dinner trays, within fifty yards of him now, swarming with cats flicking their tails. Cats that don't see Billy, don't hear his legs pushing against the bath-like water. He sees fish bones and white Chinese dinner boxes and Styrofoam cups. A black kitten chases a bug, and a gray cat pounces at what seems to be a burst of light. But the heap is unaffected. It is as grand as the Skyway Bridge, larger than any heap of garbage, the tin winking and blinking. There is nothing garbage-like about it, everything licked clean by cats, drying in the sun, sinking into the land. To Billy it is a monument like the Seminole Indian sand dunes built in recognition of the dead with bits and pieces of the dead's not-so-precious belongings, a bead, a plate, a bone.

At first he does not see the Hermit. He notices only the boat with grass growing around it. It looks like an old rowboat that might once have had a motor mounted to the back, but now the bleached wood shows beneath the paint. Then what he thought was only the brown of trees turns into a small man, as if separating from the bark of pines behind him. The tiny man is so still Billy has to gaze for a few moments before he is sure he is real. He skin looks like a composite of dirt and tar, triangles of black and brown interlocked with each other. He has never seen a human quite this color. He is sitting in the boat staring at Billy through small black eyes. Billy stops, the paper bag dangling from his hand.

The man raises a stick in the air. "Puta!" he hollers shaking the stick. A cat on the edge of the boat darts away. "Puta! No llevas puta no llevas!"

Billy holds a hand up over his eyes to stop the silver from striking him. The little man is haloed in light. He is shirtless. His shoulders are both wide and thin. He could be a condor if he spread his arms wide enough, but his chest is sallow and sunken, an old man's chest, and from Billy's distance it appears hairless. Behind the man a large white cross leans against a tree. Billy squints and shifts the hand on his forehead: it is made of 2 X 4's mounted with bleached white clamshells.

"Yo dejas! Intruso! Mi isla! Puta! Mi isla! Dejas!" The Hermit's voice is high and garbled, as if he is speaking through phlegm.

Billy repeats the words in his head. Puta. Dejas. Puta, dejas. And finally mi isla. Mi isla. They are a code, a message and today is the only day he has to retrieve this message.

"Why have I lived?" he asks finally, because this is what he needs to ask. This is what he needs to know. And there is no one, no one, who can tell him. Not his mother in the dark watching Judge Judy or waking up at 4 a.m. reciting scripture, not the high school girl he took to Wendy's for iced teas. They'd talked for hours, mostly she talked, about books and music and philosophy, about the blind spots of science and the limits of religion. They'd met on the beach at a cement picnic table where Billy had been plucking at a guitar that felt wrong in his arms. She hadn't been afraid of his pale face and pale eyes. He thinks about the girl now, briefly, her young face, her cut-off shorts, her white T-shirt, and then she's gone and there is only the reflection of the TV dinner trays glinting like fish eyes and the echo of his own voice across the lagoon, the stillness around it, as if nothing has been said and nothing has been heard.

The small man screams again. "Dejas puta! Dejas dejas!"

Billy backs away whispering the secret words to himself. Puta. Dejas. The little man stands in the boat shaking a fist. Cats run into the pines. Billy turns and wades through the thick water, listening to it part and close around his calves. "Puta puta puta!" the man shrieks until Billy enters the mangroves on the opposite side of the lagoon.

He reaches the dry sand again listening to the squelching of water squirting from his tennis shoes. On the way back to his canoe he marks the things he sees: an empty clear glass flask, an old flip flop, half a lawn chair, yellow and blue crab trap line with half a buoy, an old fishing lure, a can so sun bleached he can't tell if it was soda or beer, an orange whistle, a piece of Styrofoam, a green wine bottle, barnacle-covered plywood, remnants of a blue tarp, a TV dinner tray, and finally, his wax paper, empty, licked clean. He wads it up and throws it in the bag.

The canoe moves in place, pulling at the branch as if it is the very same movement he watched while eating his sandwich. He unties it, climbs in, and begins to paddle. The silver gunwales burn with sun. It's much hotter out in the open sunlight, and the air is thick with humidity. He strips his white T-shirt, dips it in the water, and puts it back on. He rounds the tip of the island, leaving the small hermit far behind. The wind does not pick up even though the area of water around him is larger, the islands further apart. He turns his canoe away from the island and away also from the nearby mainland where he started out this morning. A cormorant stands on one leg on a green Intracoastal marker, its black, shiny wings held open, drying in the sun. Billy looks behind him. There is a long seawall covered with overgrown grass, an open field, steely gray retirement apartments, and behind those, the surprising stretch of city.

He stands on the seawall watching himself, the face turning away from him, his head bent, his white T-shirt soaked with salt-water, his thin hair dusty, disheveled. He watches the movement of his pale arms, forward and back, forward and back. One side then the other. The sun glints against the stern of the canoe and flashes in his eyes. The man in the canoe, the self in the canoe, seems tiny going out into all that openness. There is the man in the canoe, there is another mangrove island dotted with white birds off to the right, and then there is openness, open gray silver sheen of water, turning bluish green with the day. Far off the yellow Sunshine Skyway Bridge rises out of the water on cement spider legs, glowing and golden. The boat and the man are tiny. Tiny in comparison. From the seawall, he watches himself paddle off into the nothingness.

The boat drifts past the Island of White Pelicans, and Billy rests the paddle across his knees. The pelicans are perched in the green waxy mangrove branches behind a sign in the water that says "No Trespassing, Protected Area." He thinks of the islands in the keys that are protected for the benefit of the navy who he imagines does bomb testing there. These pelicans look softer than pillows, as if their feathers were the white down of a baby bird. They are storybook creatures, like the pink spoonbill cranes that sometimes stalk the low tide flats of Intracoastal islands. The tropical nature of the place he lives surprises him—the city seems otherwise so manmade. The pelicans are the angels from the Bible stories of his childhood. He can hear his mother's gravelly voice reading to him, smell the smoke on her house dress. He used to float away when he was a boy to a world of white pelicans flying in formation above mangroves and still water, just like today. Three rise into the air and coast weightless above the gray water. Billy is not weightless. He is heavy in his boat. His arms are heavy and the paddle as it strikes the surface is heavy.

This would be a good time. He has talked with the Hermit on the Island of Cats. He is beside the Island of White Pelicans about to enter more open water. He is within an hour's paddling distance from the Sunshine Skyway Bridge. He has separated from himself. He has left a piece of himself behind to look after his mother. He opens the bag and pulls out the pills. The bottle is hard to open. He has nothing to puncture the tin foil top, and his nails are bitten and dull. Eventually, he pokes it hard enough with his pinky finger, and the finger goes through. He pulls the cotton out. This is the part that feels the most like a cliché. But there has been no better plan. What he wants most is to sleep, because even now, many hours before noon, he is tired of being awake. Tired of the heat that gathers around his eyes and on the back of his neck, tired of his swelling feet, tired of the way his arms itch from saltwater film, of the weight that falls into his bones and tugs at his muscles. His arms are weak, and they never seem to feel anything other then tired when he paddles. Each stroke, he feels no merging of himself and the water. And today, today is supposed to be a good day. He takes as many pills as he can swallow. He drinks the entire bottle of Evian to get them down. The girl in the Wendy's pointed out that Evian spelled backwards is "naïve," which is how he feels. That feeling, he supposes, is inescapable.

He listens to the blade cutting the water's surface; the silver water rolls off it like mercury, the quicksilver of time and space. The canoe is a spoon turning in light, a hook sunk deep in mud. Mercury never does stay still. In the distance, an enormous cruise boat passes under the Sunshine Skyway Bridge. Eventually, the canoe rocks from its wake. The wake is the only disturbance so far, but he knows as he gets closer to the bridge, the water will grow rougher. He imagines the people on the cruise ship eating their snacks, hors d'oeuvres in silver dishes spread out on white table clothes. He thinks about his tuna fish sandwich, but already the joy has escaped him, and what his memory recalls is the regular blandness. He thought it would be different. But already the food he's eaten tastes tired. It is a tired memory. Puta puta puta, he says aloud. His head feels heavy and light at the same time and his eyes feel as if sprinkled with cement powder, the familiar sleeping pill feeling he has learned to welcome. What a disappointment it is to wake up!

He leans toward the water, and it is green suddenly, green blue, the light reaching through the depth like a flashlight in a cave, a spidery ghost light illuminating thousands of tiny particles of dust and life. He scoops the water into his palm and wets his face and neck, but already his neck tingles with a coming numbness. The boat moves of its own accord. A shadow crosses the bow, and when he looks up, he is in shadow, at first chilly. The water is sucking and churning, spinning him, as if in slow motion, toward the enormous cement leg of the Sunshine Skyway Bridge, still over 100 yards away. He lays the red paddle down. He lies down himself, the numbness creeping across his face, even his hands tingling and disappearing. He stares into the shadow. The bow spins around into light. He stares into the light. He does not squint. It doesn't matter if he hurts his eyes. He wants to see. He wants to stare down his oppressive sun. Mercury the quicksilver of dreams and death. This collage of everything. A fish pile with garbage. Skinny cats chewing on eyes. Mi isla.

He'd planned stops along the way. He'd gotten up before dawn, his mother snoring on the couch, one strap of her threadbare nightgown, patterned with faded green flowers, has slipped halfway down from her shoulder to her elbow, revealing the squashed flesh of her breast. The house smells of cigarettes and death. He is 33 years old. He can't keep a job. The only person he's had a real conversation with in the last five years is a high school girl he had iced tea with once at Wendy's. The sun pressed against the yellowed Venetian blinds. "It's going to be another hot one," a weatherman said to a cheery morning show hostess. He'd turned off the TV. He'd left the house. He imagines the red paddle's wake disappearing behind him. First it is a line disconnected from the boat, and then it is nothing but the pattern of the water, the current spinning the surface like waves spin sand into swirls as they throw it ashore. Gray streaks spread the gray dust.